BANGFACE
and the
GLORYHOLE

ANDREW HILBERT

ISBN: 0692651608
ISBN-13: 978-0692651605

For Nina

ACKNOWLEDGMENTS

Without the book *The Case of the Missing Volkswagen* by Gerald Locklin, I don't think the character Bangface could exist. I'd like to thank my fiancée, Nina, who is endlessly supportive even as I stomp through the house, worried about everything and wondering if any of what I'm working on is any good. My folks raised my brothers and I in a household that was built on laughing until we cried. My grandmother, Donna, is a writer who I have always looked up to and who unlocked my love for reading writing. My grandmother, Teresa, came to America with my grandfather to raise their daughters in a country that had more opportunity for them even though they had to give up much to do it. Jack Arambula is my greatest collaborator and he brings my work to life visually. Austin, Texas, the city this book is based on, is my adopted home and I'm glad to have found it (just like every other Californian, *right?!*)

ONE

I went to a therapist once. She kept telling me I had to get out of my daddy's shadows. I was too busy living for "my perception" of Pa's "expectations."

Bullshit.

Pa always said a man makes his own road.

That therapist didn't know shit.

I had to start going to one – didn't want to - but sometimes when you get shot in the face after a drunken brawl in a lights out saloon and the only thing you remember is a pickled egg, the department makes you stop working until you get your emotions all figured out.

I figured it all out myself, though.

Figured I oughta quit drinking.

So I did.

It's nothing but Topo Chico for me and the occasional midnight tap water. Sometimes I'll squeeze a lime. Sometimes I'll get a soda. But that shit's bad for my teeth. The ones I have left, anyway.

It was a pickled egg that started the fight, I remember. Don't remember what about the pickled egg. Don't remember who said what. Maybe it was the last pickled egg and one of us wanted it more. I ended up shot in the face, woke up in the hospital, and didn't even remember. Motherfucker probably got the pickled egg.

Not too long after I was allowed back at work, the Chief had me doing paperwork. I wasn't built for paperwork. I was built for policing. Paperwork was for secretaries. We had our share of bowl-cutted weirdos who wore suspenders do the typing for the real detectives.

Chief says, "You ain't safe on the streets. You're a liability for now."

I turned in my badge not too long after that. Opened up my own business. I was raised on the free market, just like daddy always said. A man makes his own road.

The cases are more interesting on this side of city government, that's for sure.

Regular cops, they don't deal with the kind of shit I deal with day to day. In fact, just today, some queer walked in and was worried his partner (soon to be married, I might add; congratulations to them) was running out on him on account of the weird spiral scars all around his ding dong.

I had to google what could cause spiral scarring but then the guy says, "No, no, I shouldn't have said spirals. I should have said fractals. They glow in fuchsia and neon orange, too," he says.

Now that was a problem google could not solve.

"You got pictures?"

He got all embarrassed or something because he was looking at me like I was stupid.

"I got shot in the face," I said just in case he was

wondering why half my face drooped a little, one eye was lazy, and the droopy side was missing most of an ear.

"No, no, not that," he said. "If I took a picture, he'd suspect I suspected something."

"Does he do anything to hide it?" I asked.

"He tells me it's this new fashion like the way some ladies shave and then put crazy glitter all over themselves."

"Well, if he's proud of his John Dangler, why wouldn't he want you to take a photo?"

The queer couldn't think of anything to say to that. That's why I'm on my side of the desk and he's on his side. I pay rent here.

"Will you tail him for a night or two?"

"Woah, woah, now," I said, getting up out of my chair. "I support full rights and all that kind of jazz, but my cheeser only quesos for senoritas."

Again, he gets a look like maybe he walked into the wrong place and with a suggestion like that, maybe he did but I was willing to sit back down to hear him out. Sometimes your clients just need to talk themselves out of a case. Talk themselves into a simpler solution.

"I don't know if this thing is going to work," the queer says.

"Hey, buddy, you've been in my office for five minutes and I don't even know your name. I feel bad calling you queer but I asked a friend once and she says queer is what's preferable for people under thirty these days. You don't look a day over twenty-five."

"My name's Vince."

The queer's name is Vince.

"Vince, why won't this thing is going to work? That's what you said, did you not?" Sometimes I get to thinking that I was born to do lawyering because I like to use the exact words people say to me when I don't understand what the hell they're saying to me to get them to say it again in a different way. If I still can't figure it out, I just nod.

"This. This!"

I nodded.

He started to back away.

"Vince, before you go, just know that some cases are so interesting and so mentally rewarding that I take them pro bono. I even work them on contingency if there's loot."

He started to come back in the door. That's how I get 'em back in.

"If you have any friends that have cases you think might be intellectually stimulifying, send them my way! Please and thank you."

Vince, again, with that goddamn look like I was stupid.

This is capitalism, I shoulda said to him. Sometimes you gotta get customers by word of mouth. Some cases should be free. That way people say things like, "That guy solved my case. Check him out." Vince didn't understand capitalism. He didn't get the free market.

I read somewhere that most languages have different words for free. Like Mexican. They say 'gratis' for free. It's pretty obvious why different languages have different words for free. Free's an American word. What use is an American word for a Mexican?

Anyways, they never did catch that guy who shot me in the face. It's what I do in my free time. It's my own pro bono. Couldn't charge myself but I do deduct my expenses.

This is America and a man makes his own road. That's what daddy always said.

TWO

I guess I forgot about Vincent until another homosexual-American came in.

"Wow, two in one day," I said as the man entered. He was wearing a Hawaiian shirt and flip flops so I knew quite easily that this guy was a Californian.

"What do you mean?" he asked me.

I took a long, drawn out sip of Topo Chico because I didn't figure he could hear me when he wasn't supposed to.

"Two customers," I said and put the Topo down.

"Look," the guy says and looks me in the eye. He kind of leans over my desk like he's desperate. "A friend told me about you."

I wished I coulda called Vince right back in to show him the benefits of pro bono but he walked out leaving nothing.

"There's some weird stuff going on around town," the queer says to me.

"This is Austin, Punchy. If it wasn't weird it'd be

Knott's Berry Farm. I'm sure you're familiar."

"Are you familiar with glory holes?" He was all whispery like the CIA was watching him or something.

"Speak up," I said because I was not familiar with glory holes and, boy, once he was done explaining to me what they were, I wished I still weren't familiar but what's done is done. Now I know that a glory hole is a hole in a bathroom stall that folks use to commit anonymous sexual favors for each other.

"What if there's no stall?" I asked. Punchy didn't answer but it was simple. No stall, no glory hole. Strangers'd just have to close their eyes and not tell each other their names like they did in the good old days.

Then Punchy pulls out a few Polaroids from his back pocket like they'd been tearing his ass up. You can guess what they're of but I'll just tell you. Punchy took pictures of his ding dong and they matched the description of the John Dangler Vincent was blabbering about.

"I should call Vincent," I said. "But I don't have his number."

"You know Vince?"

"I coulda swore he said his name was Vincent," I said.

Punchy stood there with his eyes rolling.

"People who roll their eyes are stupid," I said. "You've been in here for five minutes and I don't know your name," I said, "but I don't want to know your name because I've been calling you Punchy and I think that it fits because you seem retarded. Like boxers get after they've been punched too many times over too many years."

"Do you know Vince, though? This is important."

"Know is a strong word," I said. I was getting a little uncomfortable because I don't know what he was insinuating. I live in Austin, sure, but there are still a few things I'm uncomfortable with and one of them is people asking me an incomplete question. "He came into my office and asked me to tail his partner to which I said, 'No, sirree, Comacho.'"

I must have been speaking too fast because Punchy stood there looking like his mind just left his brain.

"Vince came in here..." he said. "I can't believe he did something behind my back."

"Does Vince know you're here?"

Quick questions always did the trick in getting a stutter-stepper to eat their own tongue.

"Of course not. I..." he trailed off and looked into the corner of my office where I hung my American flag.

"It's an American flag, Poncho. Get used to it."

"I did something bad, terrible, horrible for our relationship but I fear it has more implications than just me and Vince and our soon-to-be marital bliss."

"The glory hole," I said. The words felt like warm Dr. Pepper coming out of my mouth. Gross.

"The funny thing is, when I did the deed, there was nobody on the other side. I knew this because as soon as I saw the glory hole, I hitched up my pants and went to check the other stalls. I was alone. Completely alone. I made sure of it. I'd always heard of glory holes but never got around to using one. I figured I'd just take a poke and get one thing half-assed off my bucket list."

I nodded and took another slurp of Topo.

"You didn't happen to bring any limes in, did you?" It was worth a shot. Some folks carry around limes in their pockets. Nobody I know but I'm sure some folks do.

He didn't answer. Almost like I was speaking in a foreign tongue.

"But as soon as I took a poke, I heard the sound of something like an elevator or something. And there was a pink flash from the other side and well..."

7

"Your pecker got sucked in?"

"Something like that. But it left this scarring."

He threw the photos on my desk like I should frame them just like I frame the photos of ladies in the Sunday Target ad newspaper inserts. It's hard being a private detective. Ladies don't come in near as often as fellas worried their ladies are running out on them.

Those jobs are the easiest, by the way. You just pretend like you're following the ladies and you tell the men that everything's all right. What they don't know won't hurt them and what I don't know won't risk another bullet to my gullet.

Getting shot hurts. Especially getting shot in the face. Movies make it seem like as soon as someone shoots you, you're dead. Or, if you ain't dead, you can run around like some kind of superhero with undies on the outside. Not true. I can attest to that. I woke up in the hospital with no memory and half my face on the floor. No pickled egg is worth fighting for, folks. Just my dos pesos.

"Are you even listening to me, mister?"

"It sounds like an open and shut case, amigo. Keep your wiener pointed at the toilet and all your problems are gone."

"Yeah, but…"

"No buts."

"It could be some weird government experiment. Why is the glory hole some kind of fuchsia colored portal to another dimension?"

"The simplest answer is usually the best answer, Punchy. The simple answer is, 'So what if it's a government experiment? What are you going to do about it?' This country didn't become the top dog by standing idly by while the Chinamen and the Ruskies made all of the advances. When the communists put a dog in space, we watched and waited. Then they put a man in space and we said, 'Fuck it, we're going to the moon.' We went to the moon, remember?"

"I don't think you have an answer for me."

This got me going. I was rattled.

"Now, listen here! Tell me where this aforementioned glory hole is and I'll go check it out."

"The airport."

"Austin-Bergstrom?"

"Where else?"

Where else indeed. The F1 European fans travel in and out of there all day. No wonder they brought over their glory holes to make America feel more like Nazi Germany.

"All right, Punchy. You go home to Vincent and tell him everything's going to be all right. Bangface is on the case."

Punchy looked happy and well-pleased with my answer.

Then he said, "Where'd you get that name anyways?"

"I'll need five hundred to start, and two-fifty when this case is laid to rest."

"I've only got two hundred on me."

"Fine, two hundred and that Hawaiian shirt." I'd always wanted to pretend I'd been. Hawaiian shirts are pretty expensive, if you haven't gone looking for one yet, now you know.

He pulled out his wallet and pulled out two crisp Ben Franklins. Brand new. I thought I saw a few other bills in there but they were all crunched up and I figured he'd want to get a hot dog or a burger on the way home. Figured it's better for his chances getting served if he's shirtless with money than shirtless without. I know what they do to shirtless men without money. They say, 'Get the fuck out of here, you bum.'

"Where'd you get that name? Bangface?" Punchy

asked again.

"I got shot in the face. Daddy always told me I had to brand myself. Once I left the force I started calling myself Bangface. It's more catchy than my actual name."

"That is?"

"None of your goddamned business. Now get out of here before I get Mariposa to meow at you."

I kicked the cat that hangs out at my feet under my desk. She took one look at Punchy and then fell back asleep.

"Even worse than hatred," I said to Punchy. "Utter indifference. Mariposa is well-attuned to folks, you know?"

Punchy turned around and left. His Hawaiian shirt would have to be washed. He left a huge sweat stain on the back and I hate smelling like other people.

THREE

If there's anything more stupid in the world than an airport, let me know. All Punchy had me going on was that it was a restroom in the airport. There are tons of restrooms here and I reckon a glory hole wouldn't last too long once the TSA found out about it.

Unless they did it themselves.

I read the news just like everyone else in the world and I know how the have an affinity for feeling people up through blue latex gloves. Hand condoms, we used to call them on the force for when we had roadside strip searches. I always thought the practice detestable but we did have stories for the dinner table later. Always.

If you haven't been to an airport when you're not picking somebody up or flying somewhere else, you ain't missing a damn thing. You can't get past security without a ticket so I hung out at the Delta self-check in, looking for a mark.

Families were bad news and foreigners had languages that were louder than American. I was looking for a white guy with hemp sandals and dreadlocks. I wanted to test their allegiance to their free love ethos and whatnot. Luckily, it didn't take more than five minutes to spot a hemp-sandal-wearing-weirdo. He had a duffel bag and he put it on the floor. He looked at the computer like it said his mother wore combat boots. You could see the disdain in his eyes for being forced to play the capitalism game. Free love and free travel and all that nonsense. This is America, bud, and if you want to get out, you're going to have to pay.

"Excuse me," I said as I gave him a little nudge, pretending like I was going to the next check in.

"Woah, dude," the guy said. "Respect personal space, man."

"Personal space is theft," I said because I heard something like it from a hippie drunk-type I used to drink with at the bar.

He looked at me, through his red, puffy eyes like he was on the last leg of a long flight or he was smoking old Mary Jane.

"Good thing you're in Austin," I said, gave him a little nudge, and pointed at the police officer that was chewing bubble gum. "They don't allow bubble gum on the force in San Antonio."

I could hear the whir of the machine printing his boarding pass and it was time to act. I reached over to his armpits and let out the meanest tickle I ever gave someone outside of childhood and the first time I got laid.

He was laughing and laughing and the police officer just continued to chew his bubble gum, figuring we were just the type of good-for-nothings this town is full of.

"Dude, I hate being tickled, man!"

What is this guy? Too good for being tickled? So I tickled a little harder until he finally passed out. A lot of folks don't know this but I learned it on the force. Sometimes laughter is the best method of forcible detainment. You make a guy laugh against his will and he will always remember you as the guy who made him laugh during the hardest part of his life.

I don't remember laughing when my face got shot but I'm sure if I did laugh, I'd remember. One step closer to solving the mystery, folks. It's just the way it is. Little things. Little moments of inspiration.

I took the duffel bag and his boarding pass and skated through security. It'd be awhile for anyone to notice a passed out hippie on the floor on account of nobody notices a hippie unless they can smell him. Airports are so full of Clorox and drugs-up-the-stinker that a hippie's scent is nary noticeable. But it really depends on how much patchouli the hippie is around on a daily basis. This hippie seemed all right. Maybe the dreads were just a style choice. Every hippie I've ever known invaded my personal space and didn't think twice about it even knowing full well that they are morally opposed to deodorant that works. I've tried the natural stuff. The water crystals, the vinegar solution, all that stuff. The water crystals don't work and the vinegar solution smells like vinegar. There's no fighting it. Corporations make the best deodorant.

Now, I'm not a corporatist. No, no. They took down our pants and made fun of the way our butts looked in 2009 but sometimes you just have to give credit where credit is due. Proctor & Gamble make a good product and that's why they're still in business after all these years.

I know I said I skated through security but I just want to point something out. They were all wearing blue gloves even before taking anyone aside. One could only hope they change them when the work gets real dirty. They barely even looked at my ID, either. They didn't even notice that I was far more handsome in person than the picture of the hippie on the ID.

Hell, I'm surprised he even had ID.

Maybe he wasn't a hippie.

The TSA agents were all chewing bubble gum, too. There's an old line, "He can't walk and chew bubble gum at the same time." I think it's about people who are goofy and can't multitask even the simplest things. I've got a new line. You can't protect this great nation from enemies within while chewing bubble gum at the same time. These kind of things, folks. You gotta write them down. You never know if an idea is going to make it. Write it down on a receipt and throw it away later and panic even later when you're trying to remember what you forgot. Then it'll hit you again and you'll find out it wasn't as good as you thought and you ought to just go on doing whatever it was you were doing in life in the first place.

The boarding pass said Gate C10, flying to Portland, OR. Of course. A hippie after all. I figured the toilet round there was as good as any place to start. It's a little weird seeing hundreds of 'Keep Austin Weird' t-shirts in the least weird of all places in any city; an airport. There's safety standards and stuff and you can't just go build an airport any way you like. They all look like airports. Denver has a pretty weird airport as far as airports go but you don't hear them fussing about how weird they are.

I don't know a damn thing about Denver and that's pretty weird.

"Hey," I said to a family passing me by, "You know where the poopers are? I really have to go."

They looked at me like I was crazy. The kid screamed when he saw me. I forget sometimes that my face looks like it fell off because it pretty much did.

I didn't need an answer from them, anyhow. The

pissers were practically leaking on me. I was standing right at the entrance. No wonder they thought I was crazy. Sometimes I blame my face when really the blame should be laid on my brain.

It must have been dumb luck; there's no explaining it otherwise. There were three TSA agents in there pissing away. The middle guy was pretending to pee. He was one of those afflicted with piss-shy at the trough. I can always spot 'em. I'm one of them, too. The TSA agents flanking him were staring at the wall and whistling, pissing like they were born to do it. I guess we're all born to piss. Piss, shit, and die. Everything else is pretty much learned but everyone can do those three things. Whether you do it correctly or not is irrelevant. There are people alive today that routinely shit their pants. Once, when I worked at a restaurant as a Junior Detective, I had to clean the bathrooms. You think homeless people are okay to be in an establishment and you don't want to be one of those fascists that hate all homeless people just because they like drugs more than jobs so you let them come in, buy nothing, and use the shitters.

Big mistake.

I learned that day that you can't be nice. You can't be a decent human because there is no decency in being a human, anyways. The guy made it to the toilet and left jeans full of excrement on the floor for a poor sucker like me to clean up. I took one sniff and quit.

You're never paid enough to wipe somebody's ass for them. I said, "No sir-ee, boss, you can take this job and offer it to someone else after you stick it right up your asshole."

Boss-man couldn't say nothing to that. Texas is a right-to-work state and a man can quit any job at any time for any reason. Two weeks be damned. It would've taken two weeks for me to even stick a finger on a pant leg, anyhow.

Anyways, the TSA agents kept on tinkling save for the one in the middle who was obviously wondering how long his pals were going to piss for because he couldn't go no matter how many times he said to his hose, "Go, just go, Farmer John."

"You boys know of any glory holes in this bathroom?"

The two pissers turned around and looked at me.

"Who's asking?"

I pulled out my registered private detective sheet of paper from my wallet. It was tattered and sweated on and basically illegible but the seal of the great state of Texas was there and TSA agents aren't trained to know the difference between a Whataburger coupon and a McDonald's employee.

"We've been trying to get that hole filled for two weeks."

"Well, I'm sure you don't need me to tell you that you don't need to tell anyone to fill it. Glory holes are open invitations, if you know where this melody's headed."

"You've got a pretty smart mouth," said one of them as he zipped his pants and walked towards me.

"You better wash your hands, cowboy," I said. "People already don't like being touched by you and they'd like it plenty less if they knew you were one of those types that left the toilet without running your hands under hot water for thirty seconds after soaping."

He didn't like that none too much because he tried to punch me. Luckily, I'm a frequent ducker. I duck for pretty much anything. Ask anyone who was shot in the face and survived – we don't like being hit in the face too much, though I haven't met many in the bangface club. Really, it's just me and the man in the mirror.

"You're too slow on the uptake, amigo," I said as I

punched him in the gut. He went flying back and his head hit the urinal. The pretend-pisser figured it was time to give up. He forgot to pay the bill and the city turned off the water.

"Hey," he goes like he's some tough guy, "You're assaulting a federal agent."

"Listen up, droughty, you oughta start sitting down when you pee. Helps me get the flow going every damn time. Ain't nothing wrong with knowing your strengths and weaknesses."

His face went white. Like all folks with Paruresis, he thought he was a good enough actor that nobody knew his quiet desperation. That only works with deaf folks, folks. You don't have to look at a river to know it's flowing.

"It's okay, hermano," I said and put my arm around him. "We're a silent minority. Sit down and no one's the wiser."

This sociopath, this lead actor living amongst extras, didn't like being called out on his performance. He punched me in the gut and I could feel all the air come out of me. It came out of my nostrils, mouth, and cocoa dispenser.

"That," I said in between heavy panting, "was a sucker punch, commandante!" I fell to the floor knowing that my countless hours of defensive killing training were about to come to use. I swept kicked all of those federales onto their asses and stomped the non-pisser in the stomach.

While they were busy collecting their nuts off the floor, I caught a good glimpse of the glory hole. It wasn't glorious. I wondered why anyone would stick their Jimmy Carter in that thing. Particle board does not make for a happy experience. But I suppose it's what's on the other side that counts. Still... gross.

I pulled out my phone and took a quick picture. I

made sure to email it to myself in case I was about to be hauled off to Guantanamo Bay. But these totally stupid assholes were still squirming on the tile.

I'd be back and I'd bring some protection, too.

FOUR

On the way back to my office, I felt a powerful hankering for some Cheetos. The hot kind. I could never shake my childhood love for killing my taste buds and tearing my mouth to pieces. When you're a kid, you gotta be tough. You gotta go for the most extreme of everything and by the time you're an adult, the whole world does everything it can to turn you into a sausage so you gotta cling on to the things that remind you that you were once the kid that beat up other kids for their Hot Cheetos.

Now those kids are collecting my taxes. I don't know who the winner is in that game, poncho.

I went to the clerk who was clinging on to life by bleaching her hair and drawing her eyebrows like she was never going to die. The ventilator she was attached to said otherwise.

"Hola, senorita, I'd like some Hot Cheetos and a Diet Coke."

She gave me a look. She had to. It's rude not to

look at people when you're talking to them.

"You know what, I oughta be more like you. You only live once and Diet Coke is for pussies and fatsos. Give me a Coca Cola."

"Where do you think you are… Vermont? You go pick up your own groceries and I'll ring them up. I don't leave the register."

"All right, all right," I said. "Can you point me in the right direction?"

"I don't get paid enough to point."

I never understood this mentality. Here I am with hard earned money burning holes through my better senses to buy items nobody needs. Lift a finger and point to the Coca Cola if you're one of those people. I don't mean to be disrespectful, but come on, folks. A little decency goes a long way.

Of course, I smiled and meandered my way through the aisles looking for my fix when some Confederate flag wearing Jimbo walks in with a gun. I wasn't strapped myself; I was just in an airport so I laid on the ground and prayed I didn't wet myself.

"Fill the bag, lady! I want money, beer, and a pack of Zig Zags!"

"You oughta take more than one pack, you buck toothed, good for nothing, loser worshipping, moron!"

I like to think that loser worshipping was the insult that stopped him dead in his tracks. I don't understand why people bow down to a flag that was used as toilet paper in a war they didn't win. You want respect, you back winning teams. Old Glory, friends. Old goddamned Glory. Brings a tear to my one good eye.

"What you say, friend?" He turned around and pointed his piece right at me.

"Listen to me and listen to me good, friend. You don't point a gun at something in which you do not wish to kill or destroy. Look at my face. This isn't my first gun fight."

I didn't have the best reflexes and he didn't have the best shot. He shot and hit the bag of Hot Cheetos I couldn't find. I'd have to thank him later. He did more for me than that bleach-headed breathing-corpse ever did.

"Now put down that gun and ask the lady for an application. Steady work is better than the twenty dollars you're going to get out of that register right before I send you to the slammer."

I was talking real big full-well knowing that I was on the run myself. I got a Fox News alert on my phone saying that all flights were cancelled after three TSA agents were found licking up piss off the bathroom floor. It made me a little proud, I must say. If only the powers that be knew I was just there for the glory hole and nothing more.

He shot again and hit the fridge where all the cola was. Again, this guy. This guy could really amount to something if he wasn't so dedicated to being the kind of guy that holds up ladies on ventilators at corner stores.

I stood up, confident that his shot wasn't straight enough to hit a sleeping dog.

"Put the gun down, Jefferson Davis. You obviously don't know how to use it."

Things started coming back to me. I realized that was probably the last thing I said before I got shot in the face over a pickled egg. As soon as I remembered that, he shot again and it zipped by my ear that no longer was.

I did a somersault and my leg struck him square in the zipper, underneath which hung a set of testes. It was a downward motion so it probably didn't hurt him much so I made sure to give an upward kick with my foot. His eyes nearly fell out of their holders and he fell to the floor. I took his gun, walked to the bags of

Cheetos and cans of Coke he so kindly shot at and walked to the register.

"I don't reckon you're going to charge me for these but I figure I oughta ask since you haven't said so much as a thank you since I disarmed this idiot gigante."

She smiled and started to click-clack at her register.

"Three fifty," she said.

I put down a five and told her to keep the change. I could hear sirens anyway. It was time to scram.

FIVE

It was around my fifth bottle of Topo Chico that I started to get the burps. I read somewhere that the human body registers carbonation as pain. It wasn't painful until I threw up my Hot Cheetos.

The bathroom in my office is shared with some lawyer on the same floor. He's always up to something, that guy. He used to be an assistant DA but now he works with criminals and lowlifes because he knows the system. Criminals, he always says, can pay more for their freedom than the state does for locking them away. He gets into hairy situations sometimes.

He caught me mid-puke. I was in such a rush that when I slammed the door, it didn't even shut.

"Need a fella to hold your hair?" he asked.

"Randall, enough with the nonsense and shut the door," I said.

"You're puking blood!"

"You obviously are not a fan of Hot Cheetos, friend," I said and continued my descent down the hole of the toilet.

When I was a kid, I used to imagine a dirty toilet and me picking up the dingleberries off of the porcelain and sniffing them to ensure I'd get let out of school early for puking. It worked every time. Back when I was drinking a lot, before the pickled egg shooting, I used to do the same thing. It's funny how childhood memories have a way of rearing their heads to help you in a moment of need. Sometimes you get so blocked up and bloated with alcohol but you're too used to it and your body naturally doesn't want to expel. Well, imagine a dirty toilet and sniffing some bully's dingleberries. That always helps. It's a great cure to the spins and also ensures the hangover won't be bad enough to skip a morning margarita.

When I finished wiping up the stray chunks of vomit off the toilet seat and washing my face, I knocked on Randall's door.

"Come in!"

He was sitting there with a few mean looking white kids with hair slicked back wearing suits.

"You ever hear of a glory hole?" I asked.

The kids started to shuffle in their seats like they knew exactly what I was talking about. I pointed at one of them. He was wearing a blue tie.

"You! You ever hear of them?"

"Uh, I, uh…"

"Now, now, Bangface. These kids are congressional pages. They don't associate with the joys of us commonfolk."

"Actually," the blue tie wearing dork stood up. "I've seen legislation written by the congresswoman I represent that specifically pertains to your question."

I grabbed him by the tie and threw him against the wall.

"Don't you get smart with me, Young Republican."

"I-I-I-I'm a Democrat."

"I don't care what you call yourself. Anybody wearing a tie that costs more than a Fruit of the Loom three pack at Target is a Republican. You watch yourself, chico. You stay in office long enough, and you'll become one whether you like it or not."

I was getting real sick of these bleeding heart hair slickers walking all over this town and farting out contracts to land developers. Democrats and Republicans are all the same. They grease a wheel here and there, a shelter closes, and they smile for the cameras like they just cleaned up the whole city. Now, I'm not too fond of the perpetually homeless neither but you take away a shelter and you send them all to prison and collect the paycheck the private prison corporation signed with a fancy fountain pen while you have to sign the back with your blood.

"Tell me about this legislation before I have to take a punch at my good friend, Randall, here just so you know I mean business."

"The Honorable Congresswoman Perry representing San Antonio is working on legislation to ban the unauthorized construction of glory holes in public places."

"Another assault on our freedom," I said. I pulled a Topo out of my back pocket. "Any of you got a bottle opener?"

They all looked around like they'd heard of no such thing.

"A bottle opener! You know! To open bottles with, you fucking alcoholics!"

Randall stood up.

"You need to calm down. None of us drinks while working."

"You oughta start, peckerwood! It'd give you some class."

The kid wearing a red tie stood up.

"How'd you get that name, anyway? Bangface? We were wondering when we saw the placard on your door."

"I got shot in the face at a bar over a goddamn pickled egg. Never found the guy who did it but, like Pa always said, 'You don't shoot a man in the face and live long enough to get away with it.' I'll find him, I'm getting closer and closer every goddamn day."

Nothing like throwing up to get me on the wrong side of the bed I didn't even wake up in. That's real mean and nasty if you're slow on the uptake, kemosabe.

"Now," I said taking the seat of the blue tie wearing nerd had vacated on account of me kicking his ass. "This legislation, is it pending? Is it being argued? Is it nothing more than a conversation piece you tell to your old frat brothers to make you seem more important than you are? Or, can you forward it over to my friend, Randall, here so he can forward it over to me? The longer the email chain, the more assuredly everyone goes down with me if shit hits the propellers?"

"I'll forward it, I'll forward it pronto."

"You've got a sense of urgency. I like that. You'll make a good shit-eating congressman someday."

He was typing away at his phone and within seconds I heard Randall's phone vibrate. He picked his phone out of his pocket and said, "I love when the phone vibrates," and started fingerbanging his own touchscreen. Within seconds, my phone vibrated, too. I didn't get the same affection for the feeling as he did. Pervert.

"The Bathroom Self-Love Act, HB 1389," I read aloud. "Wherein a citizen takes it upon himself to chisel a phallus sized hole in a bathroom stall, causing destruction to public lands, and does not fill said hole with anything but his own body parts."

I looked up from my phone.

"This the kind of shit you went to school for?"

School. What a crock of shit. I'm sure this kid did the Peace Corps and all that kind of jazz thinking he'd be saving starving kids and funding cars that run on self-righteousness. No, instead he's ears deep in bathroom etiquette and how people dang their dingers.

"It's an important issue when you consider the funds needed to repair said glory holes. These are funds that could put food in people's mouths!"

"One man's food is another man's Hebrew National," I said. Hebrew Nationals are really the best tasting hot dog, though. I can't help but think that the folks at ConAgra's boardroom brainstorms entertained the idea of circumcising their dogs just to drive the point home that their hot dogs were truly of Abraham's tribe. Also because of the popular toilet-brained visual metaphor that hot dogs look like wieners.

Never put it past the bohemian marketing types to pull that kind of shit. Just the other day I saw a commercial of a naked lady cleaning her ears out with Q-Tips and getting an orgasm. I don't know what I was supposed to buy the Q-Tip for and I don't know the connection they were trying to forge in my mind but I do know that my Jimmy never becomes a Jimbo when I'm cleaning my ears. Don't ask me why but I went straight to Costco and bought one of those mega-packs. It works but I don't know how or why.

"This is good stuff," I said as I continued to pretend to read HB 1389. "Real good stuff. What'd you say your name was?"

"Al," the blue tie wearing prick said as he got off the floor. "Al Soorgensen."

"What kind of name is that?"

"My great, great, great grandparents were on the Mayflower from Sweden, I think."

"And nobody made them get a more American name than Soorgensen? I don't even know how to spell it."

"There's an umlaut over one of the Os."

"Oh," I said. "Soörgensen?"

"Söorgensen."

"Ah."

Nothing made any bit of sense anymore. There was no light at the end of the glory hole. I closed HB 1389 and clicked on my camera to see the photos I took. I scrolled to my photo of the airport bathroom glory hole.

"Y'all should stay away from this one." I waved my phone around so they all could get a look without getting their greasy fingerprints all over my screen. "Something's funny about it and if my instincts are right, Homeland Security and the TSA have something to do with it. Tell the Congresswoman not to get sexually interested while she's taking a shit there."

"She wouldn't be using the men's stall."

I smacked the smart mouth across the face.

"Shut the fuck up," I said. I needed another Topo.

SIX

Not even two hours had passed until a series of unpleasant knocks came at my office door. I was sleeping underneath my desk because my old lady wouldn't let me stay home anymore because of technicalities like my name wasn't on the lease and I never paid rent and she didn't love me anymore.

I crawled out from underneath and sat in my chair and put a book in front of my face so that when I said, "Come in," whoever knocked would feel like they were interrupting me pretty awful.

"Come in!"

A lady, wearing a muumuu came in.

"Why are you reading Archie?" she asked.

Son of a bitch. Her powers of observation would make her a real fine dick.

"Evidence," I said and threw the magazine in the trash. "Useless, though. It's almost as if the writers think we couldn't figure out Jughead was dumb if they didn't name him Jughead."

"I suppose the same goes for you," she says like she didn't just eat the whole buffet at SouperSalad. It doesn't work if you get seconds of garlic breadsticks and thirds of the ice cream, lady. You're not fooling anyone but yourself and in the end, that's the saddest person to fool. "You must've been shot in the face. You think the name makes you sound tough."

Believe it or not, she was the first person to ever figure it out without me having to explain. She may have been the shooter as far as I'm concerned.

"Do you have a violent taste for pickled eggs, ma'am?"

"Pickled eggs?"

"Don't act like you haven't heard of them. They're a popular snack for drunkards, sailors, and people that live in trailer parks."

She threw her arms in the air and acted like she was going to walk out. I knew this to be the tantrum most people throw as a means to just re-grab my attention.

"I'm not a drunkard, I'm not a sailor, and I have never been inside a trailer."

"You should try sailing. You look pretty buoyant."

"Fat jokes," she said. "Original. Luckily for you I have thick skin."

I wanted to say, "I can see that," so I did.

"I learned not to hear fat jokes. I figured the person making the joke is probably dealing with their own insecurities. Insecurity that I have long conquered ever since I was in a Dove commercial."

Oh, yeah. The Dove commercial. That's where I saw this broad before. It made me swear off Dove. Making folks think it's okay to look like they eat soap when the corner store is all out of Caramellos and Butterfingers.

"Listen, lady, either you got a job for me to do or you don't. Stop wasting my time. I've got important work to do." I grabbed the Archie comic out of the trash and started reading again.

"Despite what you think," she says, she says, "Archie will never fuck Veronica. Nothing ever happens in Archie. They're just high school kids espousing the morality of a time in America that only existed in the minds of priests and Mormons."

This broad was something else. Real smart talker. I find that it's best to just nod and nod and nod while people like that talk. They'll think you're stupid, sure, but they'll never be sure of it.

"Besides," she says, "You're not as thin as you think you are."

She was right. I'd been dealing with body image issues ever since I read about it on Facebook. My chest sagged and I had weird patches of hair growing on my back and I got shot in the fucking face.

"What I'm about to tell you," she leaned over my desk, "is top secret and confidential. If I see this on the news, in the paper, or on craigslist, I'll know exactly where it came from and I'll be back here to kill you."

"Then why are you telling me if I can't tell anyone else?"

"Because some of my clients came in to tell me how great of a detective you were."

Word of mouth, amigos. Word of mouth. I never thought I'd be in such high demand these days but you get two queers in a row in one day and, hot damn, business is booming. I could see it now; a plane skywriting 'Bangface on the Case!' I wonder how much that costs. I probably know a guy.

"Your clients must be smart people to recognize a job well done. And for cheap." It was about time to raise my rates. She'd be none the wiser.

"There's a glory hole at a truck stop just outside of Elgin. My clients say it's a portal and it's run by the government. Lonely truckers go and stick their appendages in there and they come out looking like a bad acid trip. That's how government agents know where the portals are. It's all top secret, hush-hush, numbers station kind of thing."

I wrote down numbers station.

She pulled out a little radio.

"Tune this to AM 1040 at nine every night."

"Thanks, but I already have a radio." I pointed to my phone to remind her we live in the 21st century.

"Not this kind of radio." She pulled out a piece of foil from her purse and wrapped it around the antenna. "See?"

It looked like the kind of radios people who carry all their belongings in stolen shopping carts carry around listening to static. But I had to pretend to be impressed.

"Wow," I said. "Aluminum foil." Then I pointed to my phone again. "I can carry thousands of songs on here, never have to listen to some boneheaded DJ talk about Paul McCartney coming to the Harry Ransom center either."

She slapped me across the face.

"Nine every night, you Neanderthal."

"Yes, ma'am."

SEVEN

I was in my office fidgeting around with the hobo radio, trying to figure out how it even worked. I consider myself a modern man, a tech-savvy man. I like flicking things with my finger and talking to Siri and Googling things. This was like ancient technology. If Jesus had been burdened with this madness, he would have never climbed up the cross. He would've just said, "Fuck them, Daddy. Let's go to space."

Anyway, I scrunched up the foil on the antenna and rolled around the dial waiting to hear for some kind of confirmation I was on 1040 AM.

Then I heard the sound of flip flops. That's torture. Whoever was spying on me had caught on pretty good. I can't stand the sound of smelly rubbery stuff hitting sweaty feet. It sounds like rubber chickens fucking. It wasn't coming from the radio, though. It was coming from down the hall. I lunged out of my desk and grabbed an empty bottle of Topo Chico from the pile that had grown out of my recycling bin. Recycling is one of those things I don't put too much faith in. I heard a rumor that recycling glass, at least in the US of A, is a total waste. And I heard that single stream recycling, which is the very kind the city of Austin does, is inefficient. You get a piece of cardboard wet and half the stream goes to the same dump you were guilted out of throwing it in in the first place. But, you know, you gotta keep everyone happy.

I knew a guy, used to call him Big Man Japan, because he was big and he was from Japan. Taller than Shaquille O'Neal but this guy could shoot a free throw. He was an accountant. He spent some time in Japan and said they have different types of trash pickups every day. You throw your compost shit into a certain bag, paper stuff in a certain bag, glass, and the list goes on. Every day! Every day! Now that's how you're supposed to do it. But, no, no, no! We'd rather keep everyone happy. Put your recyclables here, they say. No, don't worry about separating them, they say. We have a robot that does that, they say. Turns out they want you to feel like you're recycling but they don't want you to turn off the TV to throw something into something else. It's nonsense. Big Man Japan'd have something to say about this but he doesn't speak English.

"Get up," some voice said. The voice belonged to disgusting smelling toes. I know because he kicked me in the nose before saying a damn word.

It was Vince.

"I had a dream," he said.

"Stop right there, gordito. Nobody cares about dreams. They're only interesting to you because they happened to you. I had a dream that I rode a whale through the air and landed on Jack in the Box. It was pretty fucking cool but I can tell by that mentally deficient vacancy on your face that it just sounds like beans falling into earth."

"The dream is important!"

"Turn it into a story, then. Otherwise, I don't care."

Vince pulled out a notebook and started writing. But he stopped once he realized he started to forget the dream completely.

"Don't you hate when that happens?" he asked.

"What?" I said.

"Listen, is he cheating on me or what?"

"Cheating on you, yes, if you think a particle board separating two shitting men with a hole in it is a viable partner."

Vince looked horrified.

"Glory holes?"

"There was nobody on the other side of it, as far as I know, but this goes much deeper than your grade school puppy love gumdrops hoo-ha."

"We're getting married!" Tears welled up in Vince's face like he'd just seen a real well-executed commercial.

"So am I, someday. I don't want to be alone forever." I always tried to get people to cheer up by thinking about how much worse off I am than they are. "It is better to have lost love than to love being lost, Paco."

"It's my fault… I told him I thought it was sexy."

"The stall?"

"The idea."

"Stalls have no figure. But there is the matter of payment," I said and tapped a little diddy on my desk.

"Payment? You haven't done anything!"

"He's not cheating on you unless you feel somehow inferior to what amounts to less than a wall. Would you have paid me for bad news? Because I can give it, jabroni, believe you me."

"What's the bad news?"

"Your lover is a test subject in a wide ranging government conspiracy and now I'm a target and I'm pretty sure you were sent here to kill me."

Vince looked at me all cross-eyed, shook his head, and walked out the door.

I got up and went back to the radio.

"Ah! The numbers are the stations!"

I tuned to 1040 AM. A Bee Gees song was playing. Stayin' Alive. Fitting as a condom on a banana.

I'll need some bananas.

EIGHT

Every once in a while, a man can get real down on himself and can tempt himself with drink is what daddy always said. He was a drinker and a puncher and a spitter. He'd get real drunk and punch me in the face and spit when he spoke and, boy, we all loved him. We being my ma and my brother. I kept looking up at him as my ma held me real close to her breast and my brother whimpered into my chest but I looked at him and thought, "Man, what a tough guy. Doesn't take shit from nobody. Not even a six year old kid."

So I drank a lot like daddy and got myself into real pickles. The most mysterious pickle of them all being the mystery of who shot me in the face over a pickled egg. There's an issue there, too, I remember it coming back to me now.

I saddled up the barstool and said, like they do in the movies, "Barkeep, fetch me a beer and a pickled egg."

"Fried pickles?" the kid asked. He had the tattoos

of a gang member but the face of a poet. Poets are pussies if you don't get what I mean. He looked like a pussy.

"Son," I said, "You might want to take out the little journal you keep in your back pocket to write down every little artistic fart that comes out of your b-hole because I got some reality to talk to you about."

I can get real ugly when I'm drunk.

"Why is it that a cucumber is the only thing that gets the title 'pickle?'"

He squinted his eyes and thought so hard that his brain fell out of his ass.

"There's no answer to that, son. It's just a question. You can pickle many things but you always have to denote that it's a pickled something but a cucumber, no! It must be God's favorite food because it is simply a pickle. Fuck that. I wanted a pickled egg, not no fried pickled cucumbers, so hurry it up, you son of a bitch!" I snapped my fingers and jumped out of my chair and practically hit the ceiling. I pointed to the jar of pickled eggs I had spied coming in. "There's one left, shyster!" But then my eyes followed the direction I was pointing in and I was staring at an empty jar of pickle juice.

That's where my memory starts getting fuzzy. I can remember a fuzzy looking shape eating something and laughing but if it wasn't fuzzy, then there'd be no real mystery.

"The pickle juice'll do," I should have said. Pickle juice is good for your immunity, daddy always said. He drank a lot of it. Ate a lot of pickles. Pickled a lot of things. Ma and his girlfriend always called him the Pickle Man. His girlfriend always giggled about it but ma always said it like she hated him.

About this time in my recollections, I get a real strong hankering for a Topo but a man can be addicted to Topo, too. Addiction ain't good. Topo can give you acid reflux like a motherfucker. Don't let anyone tell you that sparkling water is safe. You're rolling the dice, amigo. You're rolling the dice.

NINE

My head was in my Archie comic when I woke up. I heard some serious pounding on the floorboards out in the hall outside my door so I shot up. Things were getting real, folks. Real real.

I could see the feet of someone standing outside my door. Then, a folded envelope slipped through. Then, of course, the feet stomped away again.

I waited to make sure they were gone.

"Mariposa! Mariposa!" I kicked the cat. "Go sniff around and see if there's any danger!"

Unbeknownst to most folks is that cats have a real keen sense of smell. Almost ten times stronger than a dumb ass dog's. The only difference between cat's smelling ability and a dog's is that dogs love their owner enough to use it. Mariposa looked up at me and closed her eyes and put her head back into her fur. Cat's don't give a shit about wasting their talents. Their wholes lives are about wasting talent once you give them food and a place to sleep. I suppose that's the goal of all living things. I can't speak for trees, reptiles, birds, or insects, though. I understand mammals.

"Good girl," I said to Mariposa, still begging her after eight years for some kind of symbol of her appreciation of my ability to bring her food. No luck. Mariposa's a fucking bitch. And I'd be a liar if I said I didn't love her for it.

You gotta take things as they are, folks. You go running around looking for the belt you lost, you're going to look down and see you lost your pants along the way. Nobody likes being caught with their pubes in full view. Forget the belt. Fold up your waistband and hope to find a belt later in the day. That's what daddy always said when we hid the belt from him and that's advice that is applicable in all of life. That's the kind of parenting that is in decline these days, folks. You let your kids run around and be too free and all of the sudden they grow up to be asking folks on the street for money and how to get where they're going. A man makes his own road. A woman does, too. I may be old fashioned sometimes but I still appreciate a Vanilla Coke.

The envelope was unaddressed. No postage stamp so the stomper sure as hell wasn't the mailman and if it was, I'd have to tell him that underneath my door is no mailbox. The mailbox is in front of my office. I'm tired of telling folks how to do their jobs.

I turned the envelope over. Lipstick. Sealed with a kiss. Maybe it was my old lady telling me she was tired of whoever was telling her he loved her and I could move back in with her to help pay the rent. That'd be something.

I opened it up and inside was a map of Elgin with a big circle on some intersection. In lipstick, a very manly form of handwriting wrote: GLORY HOLE. GO!

Things were getting more tangled. The last broad

that told me about an Elgin glory hole was a former Dove soap model with a salty attitude. This handwriting obviously belonged to a man. Unless I was letting my last century prejudices get the better of me, two people were trying to get me to go to the same place.

Hell, then I oughta go.

I've found the best form of detective work is to follow your nose. That's how all mammals get around. When it's dark, they sniff for clues of danger. Sure, you bastards are thinking, 'What about hearing and touching?' That sounds a lot like a romantic relationship to me, folks. And that's a sure as shit way to land yourself into some danger. You ever see dogs sniff each other's butts? You ever see a dog fall in love over it?

I never did.

Bet you didn't neither.

I observe for a living.

Ain't no trouble in smell.

I got up and set for my car.

TEN

The Elgin truck stop was no place to bring a date unless your date had a hankering for Hot Cheetos, Mountain Dew, and being leered at by a man who looked fit for a mortician's makeover.

"Whaddaya here fer?" The man made of wrinkles and a lack of teeth spit at me, without even looking over the titty mag he was reading.

I pulled out my driver's license and showed it to him. It was the standard issue Texas driver's license so there was no reason for him to believe the gusto of authority I threw it in his face with.

"That's yer name? Yer momma musta been real creative-like, son."

"I go by Bangface," I said and pointed at my face. "Somebody shot me. A man chooses his own road."

"So what's this mean here? You want liquor, pussy mags, or cigarettes? Yer ID is all that says to me, sonny."

I took a quick glance around the interior for

possible escapes. Never underestimate a potential sparring partner. The man looked like he drank a lot of milk despite the look of the bones his skin was hanging from. The only escape was the entrance. That'll do, though. Easiest way to get out of a place is to turn around.

"I'll take a pussy mag," I said. I needed to learn more about Mariposa anyways.

"What's yer fancy?"

"Cat," I said. "Cat Fancy."

He looked at me like I was swinging hot dogs on a string.

"When I say pussy mags, sonny, I mean the fish kind."

"I don't own any fish, sir."

He threw down a copy of Hustler.

"This'll do," I said. "Where's the shitter? I've been driving too long not to drop a deuce, Pachinko."

"Behind the Bud Light display." He went back to reading his titty magazine and paid me no interest as I collected my Hustler and went to the toilet.

I don't think I need to say this twice but just in case you're dense, here it goes. The restroom was no place to rest in. It stunk like the toilet hadn't been flushed in years and the toilet looked like it, too.

But I had to get to the bottom. That's the only way to do things.

I'll say it again. The restroom stunk. It was no place to get your dangle dingled but some folks like it that way, I guess.

I went into the first stall and there it was. It was a hole about dick-high, cut in a circle-like shape with graffiti surrounding it that is best unmentioned in polite company. There were weird stains like pee and poo-poo all over it and other things that blend quite well with a white stall. If you can't see the mess, there is no mess.

That's how I treated bathroom duty at every job I ever had. That's what old Wrinkle Face must've wrote in the employee handbook, too, but with an addendum: don't clean it anyhow.

About sniffing and the sense of smell: I know I went off on my high horse sounding like a jackass about how the sense of smell is the highest of evolved creatures. Well, there's more to it than the simplicity I sometimes convey. There's no use putting your nose in something when a finger'll do.

So I poked the hole.

Instantly, a pink cloud started seeping through the hole accompanied by the sound of an adult male giggling being obstructed by something in his mouth. That obstruction was my finger.

Quick as a second turns into another second, I jolted my hand back. My finger was wet.

Gross.

My finger had some weird spiral burns that flashed colors I haven't seen since the days I dropped acid before elementary school with a gang of toughs.

I peeked through the hole, making sure my face had enough distance from the wall so that I wouldn't have to cut my whole face off to get rid of whatever stall transmitted diseases rested there. There was nothing but the next stall's shitter in view.

"Interesting."

I got out of the one stall and into the next. There was no giggler. There was nothing but me and toilet paper on the floor. It was surprising that the toilets were as well stocked as they were. You figure a guy who can't clean his toilets wouldn't make sure there was enough TP for what lonely sojourner may come in. That was noteworthy, folks. I wrote it down on my palm for later if my sweat didn't smear it into illegibility.

I stuck my finger on this side of the hole and there

was nothing. No pink smoke. No giggling. Just a finger sticking out of a hole into another bathroom stall. Nothing to write home about.

I went back to the other side of the stall and stuck my finger in it again.

"Ouch! You motherfucker!"

With my finger still in the hole, I figured there was enough space for me to see through. There was a red and irritated looking eye staring back at me.

"State your name and your purpose!"

"I'm just looking for the end of the hole," I said. "As one is wont to do in these situations, Bob."

"This is a classified glory hole. Forget you saw this."

I poked him again in the eye for good measure.

"There's no such thing as a classified glory hole. It's here in the open and begging to be filled," I said.

I turned around and started to walk out. A hand reached out the glory hole as the very fabric of space started bursting waves around me. The hole became human sized and a man in a black suit and tie stepped out of it.

"You're under arrest."

"Under what authority?"

He pulled out his driver's license but it looked a hell of a lot like an FBI badge.

"I don't believe it. I don't believe for one second an FBI agent is looking for a good time in Elgin."

"I was in D.C. and you assaulted a federal agent with your finger."

"Don't go looking through holes you don't want to get poked through, my daddy always said."

He was a little dumbfounded, I could tell. It was a head scratcher to him because he was scratching his head. I have a way with words like that. I can disarm an opponent through superior intellect. As he scratched his head I grabbed his tie and dunked his head in the toilet.

"What's going on?" I asked. "What is the purpose of this?"

I pulled his head out of the disgusting water and gave him time to catch his breath and other folks' piss.

"We're building a high speed transport system. These are classified experiments. You kill me, you kill progress."

Progress is overrated, folks. I never rode a horse and I think it'd be more fun than driving a car. A hell of a lot more fun than sticking my broomstick in a dustpan.

Luckily for Agent Finger Food, I was no murderer.

I dunked his head again and flushed the toilet because every movie I'd ever seen had some guy doing that to some twerp and I never got the chance to do it in real life.

That was a mistake, folks. A toilet gone unflushed for that long is bound to back up and back up is what it did.

There was a lot of gurgling on behalf of the toilet and Agent Bad Breath. To my own amazement, the agent never took his head out of the water. He just kicked his legs in ways that defied gravity and swung his arms around as his face became an integral part of shit stew.

Water sloshed out from the sides of the toilet and onto the floor. I felt bad, I did, I felt real bad so I grabbed Agent Shit Head by the ears and lifted his head out.

"I'll tell you everything," he said. "Just don't kill me."

"Wasn't planning on it, Paco."

It was an effective tactic, sticking someone's head in a toilet. No wonder so many TV bullies did it. I should've asked the agent for his lunch money.

"Let's get you cleaned up."

ELEVEN

It was a quiet drive back home to Austin. Agent Bad Breath didn't want to talk too much until he got "at least three more showers," he said. That was all he said. I suspect he ain't the type to talk much anyway.

I wasn't in the mood for flapping gums neither, though. I was sneezing up a storm. Just recently switched from the store brand Zyrtec to the store brand Claritin. Some armchair pharmacist I know said that's the only way to beat allergies here. You gotta keep them on their toes.

Well, it was a bunk plan. I'm sneezing the taint into my asshole the whole way home and my eyes are itching so much that most folks think I'm crying at the song on the radio.

Ain't no song good enough to make me cry while I'm driving. Driving's a privilege; not a right, folks. Save the emotions for later. Go home and accuse your lady of ignoring you. Go home and call your mommy. Can't do a damn thing about sneezing though. Taxi Driver had a line in there about it. That's the only time your eyes come off the road is when you sneeze. I bet if you could avoid it, they wouldn't allow you to take your eyes off the road when you sneezed but you can't avoid it so they make exceptions. Even the hardest driving cab owner knows that.

This message-board-pharmacist I know once told me to go down to Whole Foods and get some stinging nettles pills. He kept saying it was "homeopathic" and "what it does is it blocks a histamine reaction." He kept saying this like it was the smartest sounding shit any elephant had ever dropped. Me, too. I look back and imagine myself nodding my head like a moron, really listening to this guy talk and I get embarrassed.

What an asshole I was to believe this guy. It ain't ever about what's said, it's all about how it's said. We're in our own 1984, folks. 2+2 does equal five if a guy says it in a way that sounds smart.

I went all around Whole Foods looking for this stinging nettles bullshit. Couldn't find it. I asked some teenager that worked there about it. He said they were all sold out but he went on and on about how "what it does is it blocks a histamine reaction." I realized my mannequin-pharmacist friend was just aping everything some teenager said and because I don't like teenagers on principle, I didn't take it seriously. That's when the walls on my phony pharmacist friend came tumbling down.

But it doesn't end there, folks. I wished it did, too.

I went home and read on the box of my Claritin box (I was still using brand name back then before a friend told me that the store stuff usually comes from the same line), and on it it said very clearly: ANTI-HISTAMINE.

You don't get to say "it blocks a histamine reaction" when you can just as easily say "anti-histamine." Beware of your friends that take five words to say something that takes one hyphenated word.

I know I can be a blowhard sometimes, too, but shit, some people. You know what I mean.

"We have to pull over," Agent Shit Talk said.

"Why is that?"

"I just saw the sign for another portal."

"And what sign is that?"

"Rips and tears in the fabric of the universe. Pink smoke emanating from the roof of the building. A splitting of the universe. Small things. Burger Kings become Burger Kangs and nobody ever knows any better. 'It's always been Burger Kang,' they say. In one universe, yes. But when a portal is created and accessed, universes collide. A few people will say, 'No, I'm pretty sure it was Burger King.' But that's it. That's the only trace of truth in the new universe we created."

"Slow down, cowpoke. Burger Kang?"

"It was just an example. Remember that book about the bear family? The Berenstain Bears?"

"Yeah."

"Spell it."

"B-E-R-R-Y-S-T-A-I-N."

"What the fuck?"

I never was a good speller and I didn't appreciate him calling me out on it.

"What do I care about some kid book, anyway?" I said, eyes still on the road.

"Some folks remember it as being spelled 'B-E-R-E-N-S-T-E-I-N.' But now, all of the sudden, it's B-E-R-E-N-S-T-A-I-N. This is a very real example of how the portals are crashing universes together in very small ways."

I had a mind to just kick this crazy person out of my car. I heard bums with dried boogers in their beards tell better sounding nonsense than that.

"Where'd you see the pink smoke?"

My better senses kicked in, though. I had a nose for investigation and this psycho talk piqued my Texas interest.

"MacDonalds."

"McDonalds?"

He looked at me like I was stupid but sure enough, the freeway exit sign said 'MacDonalds.'

"It wasn't always spelled that way. Maybe it's a rip off that Ronald McDonald hasn't found yet."

"It's always been spelled that way and that's exactly my point," Agent Confusing said.

I got off on that exit.

TWELVE

"Things are more freaky than just a Mc turning into a Mac, Lefty," I said to the agent as I stuffed some French fries down my mouth. "Look at that menu up there." I pointed.

"What? Seems normal to me."

"They're selling Whoppers instead of Big Macs."

The agent nodded and took out a pencil and paper and started writing something down. He covered what he was writing with one hand and kept looking up at me like he was drawing my portrait. I didn't ask for no fucking portrait, Poncho.

"What the hell are you scribbling down there?"

He ignored me. His thick rimmed glasses fogged up and his cheeks turned red.

"Tell me what you're scribbling and I won't dunk your head in the treasure boxes in the ladies' restroom."

He grabbed his pencil and broke it in two. Rage filled his eyes and they looked like they were just about to pop out of his head. He was sweating and convulsing and talking like a Chinaman would if a Chinaman was imitating an American racist stereotype of Chinaman tongue.

There was a curly-red-haired-patchouli-smelling-bearded hippie eating Chicken MacNuggets right behind the Agent-Turned-Red. I hate these people. You know he's probably a glass blower at home. He dabbles in it. Makes a pipe here and there and then doesn't even sell it. He stuffs it with the devil's grass and uses it for himself then complains to all his friends how an artist can't live off of his art. Glass blowing, amigos, is rarely an art. Especially if you're not selling any of it.

Imagine if one of his friends saw him eating at MacDonald's – the hypocrite! The friend would have to back out slowly and not mention it to our glass-blowing-pot-smoking walking petition and pretend he got lost on his way to Whole Foods. The whole thing makes me sick. The blatant hypocrisy!

"I'm going to say something."

"You're not going anywhere!" The Agent said with steam blowing out of his nose and ears like he was a bull on Looney Tunes.

"I make the rules here, amigo."

I stood up and went to the glass blower but the very minute I opened my mouth to extoll the virtues of the free market and how glass blowing has untapped market potential specifically because the types of people who blow glass are just as lazy as the people who suck on blown glass – be smarter than that, be smarter and be happier and be American, dammit - he disappeared.

This was no monkey in and out of a hat trick like you're used to seeing on the internet. This was no disappear behind a blanket of smoke act. His body flickered on and off and turned strange colors. His face fell into a million frozen places and then immediately collapsed on itself.

"You're not going anywhere," the agent said. "You recognize the tears and flitters in space and time and we need to study you to better our transport system."

I felt a little proud.

"Was that what you were scribbling about over there?"

The agent said nothing for a while.

We just stood there. In the middle of a MacDonald's. Where we could order Whoppers.

Then he said, "I am being remotely controlled. My body is but a vessel. My soul, my essence, has been scooped out of me entirely and I am merely a vessel of technological progress."

"You should think about writing poetry. I know some folks. They can point you in the right direction."

"Quiet."

Two men came out of the restroom and back to the ladies who were waiting on them. They seemed friendly on the way out of the bathroom so it was surprising to see them go to separate tables with not so much as a good bye.

"You wait here, Essence," I said to the vessel of technological progress. "I've got some gumshoeing to do."

I went to the aisle in between the couples' tables and stood there whistling.

"What the fuck are you doing there, whistling like some kind of child molester?"

"I was curious," I said, "about the fact that you two exited the bathroom having obviously shared something inside but then came here like strangers. What is it?"

One of the ladies looked around, leaned in towards me, and whispered, "This is how we get off sometimes. We meet strangers on craigslist and find glory holes and use them."

"Is this some kind of joke? What's wrong with the

regular in-out?" I put the pointer finger of my right hand through a hole made from my pointer finger and thumb on my left.

"It gets boring sometimes, don't you think?" The other lady said.

"I never got bored with it."

As soon as I said that a thought took a shit on my brain. Maybe I wasn't having enough to get bored with it.

"Eh, to each his own," one of the ladies said. "I think it's sexy to know that my man is with another man through a stall in a MacDonald's."

"Yuck." I couldn't help but say it, folks. Nothing was gross until she said 'stall in a MacDonald's.' That's where I draw the line. Upgrade to a Chipotle. Treat a stranger with some dignity. Hell, treat yourself with some dignity.

"Don't judge, man," the guy who called me a child molester said.

"You just called me a child molester and now you're telling me not to judge?" I was well-pleased with that verbal kung fu. He was quiet. "Let me ask you, did you notice anything weird about that glory hole?"

"Yeah, man. That's why we come here. There's a glory hole enthusiasts subreddit and there are some glory holes that give you the craziest trips. Man, I always get stamped with some psychedelic shit on my dick. My lady loves it." He put his arm around his woman and she giggled.

"This is weird," I said and shook my head.

My case was going nowhere. It was obvious Vince and his man were caught up in something they never intended to be caught up in. There was no case anymore between them. Nobody was cheating on anybody. I say for cheating to occur, it has to occur with something more than an inanimate object. If you feel insecure around a bathroom stall, then there's not much I can do for you.

They owed me money, though. No answer is better than a bad answer and it takes the same amount of work.

"All right, Bangface, let's go."

I felt the cold metal of handcuffs around my wrists. Was it all over?

THIRTEEN

"You're not going to throw me in the slammer without letting me piss are you? That's inhumane! The Chinese don't even do that anymore!"

"You and your obsession with the Chinese!" was the last thing I heard before I was served a healthy portion of knuckle sandwich.

"Can't I at least call my old lady?"

"Somebody loves you?" the agents all stood around and laughed as they kicked me in the ribs over and over again.

"She used to, I think, a while ago," I said.

"Say her phone number and we'll gladly make the call."

Who memorizes numbers anymore? These guys were building the freakiest high speed transit system history has ever known and they're acting like nobody has cellphones and keeps an address book on them.

"I don't know her damn number!"

"Then it's not love."

Kick.

"What do you know about love?"

The kicking stopped.

All of the agents stopped laughing, chewing gum... they stopped doing everything. They just stood there dumbfounded at the epiphany that they didn't know what love was.

Then the kicking started again.

"Unimportant!" One yelled.

"Who cares?" Another yelled.

"Let me go pee," I said as I hugged myself into a ball on the cold floor of whatever CIA torture chamber I was being held in.

A door opened. Light filled the room, illuminating the six mean CIA agents who continued to kick me.

"You keep kicking me and you're going to have a lot of pee to clean off your slacks, muchachos!"

"Let him pee."

It was a familiar voice.

"Vince?"

The six agents stopped kicking and turned toward Vince. "You know this guy?"

"Yes, I know him. He was finding out if my lover was running out on me. I should have known better. I saw that he stumbled upon one of our portals. I was jealous. I should have known better than to involve a third party. But there it was. The fuchsia stained markings of cuckolder. I had to know if he was cheating on me, America's technological progress be damned!"

"Hey, Shakespeare," I said, "Can I use the pisser?"

"But now he knows too much, this Bangface. And something's got to be done about him."

"I'd be glad to brainstorm once my head's all clear. I'm all full of piss and blood and probably kidney stones after all that kicking."

"Shut up," Vince said. "Shut the fuck up."

"You still owe me, by the way. No answer is better than a good answer."

"Do dead men pay debts?" Vince asked.

"I suppose not."

"Then dead men are owed nothing." Vince turned around. "Don't let him out of here alive."

The door slammed.

FOURTEEN

When I was a kid I always wanted a Slip N' Slide. We couldn't afford one though so my brother and I made do with trash bags and a garden hose. Usually we'd just end up beating each other up with a garden hose because the trash bags never did hold up too long. There's a reason a Slip N' Slide was invented and it wasn't entirely frivolous like most communists in America today like to critique. It's hard as hell to make one yourself and the market is children. Chinese children can make Slip N' Slides all day long, they get paid to do it. American children can't do it all. So American kids pay Chinese kids to do it and we're all the better for it.

This is America, kiddos, get used to it.

Daddy always thought we were wasting all of our time looking for fun.

"Learn how to have fun with a hammer," he'd say as he waved one around. "Soon this is the only thing that'll make you enough to buy all the pickles in the world and send them down the throats of an ungrateful family."

He was always philosophizing about the way of things, the way of the world, and why it was all always going to Hell. It wasn't the Chinese too much back then. They were there, sure, hanging around every corner waiting to put daggers in the backs of good American children but back then, back when I was learning about boners and how to hide them, it was Saddam Hussein and the East Germans.

"They do everything cheaper," he would always say, "and they don't even know how to sell what they make."

At night, he'd sit at the dinner table by himself. His friends liked vodka. It goes with everything. These days nobody cares about what vodka represents. He hated vodka. It could've come dripping from a supermodel waving a gun and a flag and he'd still refuse the stuff.

"I refuse the drink of my country's enemies and I expect they do the same for whiskey."

He sat alone at that damn dinner table drinking whiskey a and eating the eggs he pickled.

It takes, at the very fucking minimum, two weeks to properly pickle an egg. A good pickled egg has the consistency of cheese. He'd drill this into my head as he made them.

"You need to do things, son. But you need to do them right. Too many folks are running around selling water and calling it beer. Too many folks selling portobello as magic shrooms. A pickled egg is a fucking pickled egg because it's a pickled egg not because of what anyone says about it."

He'd sit there drinking whiskey and eating pickled eggs and pontificating about the world until he fell asleep in a puddle of his own sweat and drool.

"Nobody does anything right anymore," he'd say.

I sat on his lap, listening to it all, while my brother

and ma caught some shut eye.

FIFTEEN

All them memories must have done something crazy for me because while I was passed out, I must have started pissing. There were agents all over the goddamn place, wet as a truck stop bar whore, slipping all over themselves.

I got up, still handcuffed and hopped around giving them all a good kicking in the ribs. An eye for an eye, amigos.

Vince was gone and I figured the mirror in front of me was a two way. I gave a good middle finger to it after I checked my hair and put on one of the agents' hats. I've always wanted to wear a hat but I get too self-conscious. Daddy always said that hats were for dandies and Democrats. I knew plenty of fine Democrats and I admired dandies for dressing the way they did knowing full well there were folks running around who would kick their ass for it. I kept the hat. It was a piss soaked souvenir of taking down the federal government, even if only for a minute.

"Which one of you goons has the keys to the cuffs?" They were squirming in a circle and I kicked each one in the stomach, one by one.

"Vince has the keys! Vince has the keys! He's

probably at the headquarter hole!"

I grabbed the tattle-tale by his tie and lifted him off the floor. His feet slipped and slid but he was being held up by the force of me choking him to death.

"You're coming with me," I said. I was uncomfortable with how mean I felt but sometimes a private dick has to be a dick. Things were getting too deep and I didn't know what I'd do in a world where MacDonald's sold Whoppers. Things needed fixing.

Once he stopped slipping around on the piss on the floor, he said, "Fuck you! I'm not going anywhere!" and grabbed me by the cuffs and flipped me over onto my ass. "Get him, boys!"

But the boys were still slipping around and even though I was on my ass, I had the perfect angle for a quick up-down kick on his dollar and coin purse.

He fell to the ground clutching his dangler and I scrambled up. You ever try doing things with your hands tied behind your back? You ever try opening a door? Damn near impossible. Especially when the guy you just turned from an outie to an innie, was blocking the damn door.

"Would you please squirm a little to the left, amigo?"

It was too late. He was throwing up and his eyes were rolling back in his head.

I'd never kicked a man so hard that he had a seizure. All's fair in love and war, folks. There used to be the schoolyard rule that it wasn't right for a man to kick another man in the coin purse. Whoever made up that rule has never been in a fight. Fights aren't some honorable affair where the winner knows he's won and the loser knows he's lost. Rarely does either side know where they stand. They can go on forever and they can end in death. It's a lot easier to kick and scram.

I got myself up and walked backwards to grab the

door handle. It was unlocked.

Crouching down wasn't my thing. My knees pop a lot. You think when you're younger that you're never going to get old and you're never going to have to hold your breath to pop out a shit and you're never going to have to pop pills to get hard but it happens one day. Didn't happen to me yet.

My knees just pop. Popping's no good for sneaking.

I had to crouch, though. The windows were big in this building and there were people in suits looking around all the time. It was like they had a high risk prisoner or something.

The Man Who Knew Too Much.

That's me, brother.

"Hey, you!" some guy in white scrubs with a mask over his face said to me from down the hall.

I turned around like he was talking to somebody else.

"You, stupid!"

Nobody calls me stupid. I didn't say a word. I was covered in piss, I was pissed off, and I was going to lick the piss out of this guy. I stood up and leaned forward in a sprint. My knees popped, of course, and everyone on the other side of the mirror stopped what they were doing to watch me lunge at whitey.

He fell to the ground and I put my thumbs in his eyes, straddling him like a sorority girl on a mechanical bull.

"Get me to Vince," I said.

He didn't say anything in English. His eyes were taking a good look at the inside of the back of his head. I'm mean.

Like I said, you have to win a fight to win a fight. There's no winning in turning around out of mercy. The other guy's not going to show you mercy if you're turning his nutsack into a pussy or his eyes into tonsils. Revenge is a bitch, friends. Ensure it doesn't happen. That's my motto, anyway. It's always worked out.

Except for getting shot in the face.

"Hey, hey, hey," a soothing voice from an intercom above said. "No need to fight, Mr. Face. There's absolutely no need. We understand your frustration. We just want to understand something about you. Please get off of our dentist."

"He called me stupid and where I come from, you don't just get away with that."

"Dr. Crockett, please say sorry to Mr. Face."

I took my thumbs out of his eyes. People tend to lose their speech when you're fucking with their eyes like that.

"I'm, I'm, I-I-I-I," he struggled to say.

"I'll take it, Lefty!" I got off him.

"Good, good. Thank you, Mr. Face. Please follow Dr. Crockett to his operating room. We have new information about your facial injury years ago and your heightened space-time perceptive awareness."

"You know who shot me?"

"In due time, in due time."

Dr. Crockett hobbled toward his room. He wasn't exactly happy to be fixing me up on account of the eye gouging but I do have a move called the tappen that he should be glad I didn't pull out of my ass.

SIXTEEN

Dr. Crockett seemed like the kind of guy you could drink a six pack with. He liked to laugh, he was a little fat, and he had framed, blown up photographs of Lone Star in his office. He wasn't the kind of doctor you'd want working on your mouth. But it was the CIA. They had the best of the best and so on.

His hygienist was another story. He was a skinny motherfucker. He had tattoos and a mustache that was painted on his lip. He was too young for that. He wasn't European enough, either. But he smelled like the unshowered mess a Frenchman might be.

"This guy going to wear gloves?" I asked pointing to the hygienist.

"Mr. Face, this is the CIA. Of course he's going to wear gloves." Crockett looked over me in the chair with a big blue napkin around my neck to his hygienist with a look that said, "Put on your gloves." It was a look with his mouth because he actually said it.

The hygienist grumbled and rolled his eyes but then he slapped on some gloves.

"What's his name?" I asked right before Crockett jammed a finger into my mouth. It tasted powdery.

"Imuhtasun latex, eh? I'm not uhlerjet."

"I am," Crockett said with a fire in his eyes that worried me that he enjoyed whatever kind of torture he was going to send me.

Life is a series of getting ups and getting downs. Just a second ago I was jamming my thumbs into this guy's eyes and now he's got me getting weirded out by his hygienist while he pokes around my mouth.

"Aren't there tools designed for this?"

"Why use a tool when a finger is perfectly good?"

"I have a similar saying," I said.

"Shut up."

My eyes got real heavy and I could feel myself thinking about how MacDonald's used to McDonald's and wondering what Burger King served if they served anything at all.

"Tacos," said the soothing intercom voice. "Burger King sells tacos."

Then I thought, "What about Taco Bell?"

"Taco Bell?"

I could live with that.

SEVENTEEN

When I woke up, I was on a cold, metal table with a bright light shining on my ding dong.

"What's that got to do with anything?"

Dr. Crockett was there with his weird hygienist poking their fingers around my mouth while a very tall man in a top hat took notes while looking at my double scoop ice cream cone.

The man in the top hat looked up at me and grinned.

"You ever been shot in the face?" Dr. Crockett asked.

"Where do you think I got the name, bozo?"

"There's a piece of shrapnel lodged into the roots of one of your teeth. It's a very interesting artifact in that it seems to have been dipped in mercury," Crockett said.

"And why does that matter to me? Why am I naked? And who the fuck is that weirdo in the top hat staring at my clucking rooster?"

Then the man with the top hat smiled a real big, shit-eating grin. His teeth were all gold capped and he stood up.

"You're a Sense-Being," he said.

"Oh, don't start with that hippie shit, please," I said because I've had it up to my goddamn ears with the hippies around town these days. They put up their peace signs and they smoke weed and they wear hemp sandals and they say things like, "Dude," and, "Oh, yeah?" and they just stink up the whole town.

"No, no, no," the man in the hat said. "It's a term we use for people who are very perceptive to the subtle changes in our universe as we perfect our high speed transport system."

"Listen, Moses, I've got a few beans in my brain that taste good enough to know you're full of shit. Where are my pants?"

"Let me put it into terms a person like you can understand: the bullet that fucked your face up is allowing you to see the changes in our universe. I, too, remember Taco Bell. And I remember when MacDonald's was McDonald's and I remember when the BMT at Subway stood for Big Mass Transit."

"I don't eat Subway, chico." I gave him a kick to the mouth and I slipped off that table. Crockett put his dukes up like he was a drunken Irishman at his co-worker's daughter's quincenera. "Put 'em down, doc. You don't know what I'm capable of."

The hygienist looked mighty uncomfortable staring at me standing up in my birthday suit. I'm not ashamed of what the good Lord gave me. I could kick his ass ten times easier if he was uncomfortable with the kind of feelings I was inspiring in him, anyhow.

But the dentist didn't put his dukes down. I've warned far superior opponents than this C minus dental school student and sent them to the plastic surgeon to outfit them with new pussies after I emasculated them on the field of battle. You see, folks, a man who's been shot in the face and survived is not the kind of man you want standing in front of you naked in some back alley CIA operating room.

I once took karate lessons from a Mexican fella named Villareal here in town. He told me, "Karate, man, is more about the noise than the kick, man."

I took that to heart, Villareal, may he rest in peace. I accidentally killed him with the very spin kick move he taught me. His family was very kind and understanding and didn't sue me at all.

It takes a real master to do that spin kick naked, though.

I put my hands up and concentrated all of my energy at Crockett's eyeballs. Then I leapt in the air and spun around with my leg extended. You really appreciate what underwear does for you in times like these. I was spinning, my nuts were banging against my taint, while the President flopped around and knocked me a little off balance if I do say so myself. But my foot hit exactly where I wanted it to hit: Crockett's big dumb fat ass face. I swear to you, every tooth in that mouth hit the wall behind him.

But I wasn't done, no. This was no regular spinning kick where the foot only hits the target once. I spun so damn hard I hit him two more times in the mouth.

You're going to think I'm joking, I know it, but it's the goddamn truth. His fucking lips fell off, his gums separated from his mouth, and he fell to the floor screaming and crying and he was trying to talk real good but his tongue was wrapped around his uvula.

"Hope you have insurance, doc. Because you're going to need an x-ray on that mouth and according to every bill I've ever got from a dentist, it's a lot of fucking money."

I didn't feel too good about rubbing in how low I thought of him and his whole profession, no offense to any doctors out there, but this was a man who spent his time poking inside my mouth with some weirdo hygienist who was too skinny to have tattoos. Don't tattoos leach nutrients out of you? That's what I heard. That's why I don't got 'em.

The hygienist.

He was still there, cackling like a German psychopath who wears nothing but leather. He was real confused. Here his boss was, the Tooth Master now totally toothless, crying on the floor.

"It must be tough looking at the man you respected swallowing his own gums as he picks up his teeth off the floor," I said, not sure of what I was getting at. He was one of those guys that kind of laughs at other people's tragedies because he was certainly laughing pretty loud but I could sense fear in that cackle. A good detective can always sense fear. You could say I was a Sense Being.

"Hiiiiiii-ya!" I said as I jumped through the air karate chopping with abandon, landing a few good hits to his forehead and cheek bones.

He fell to the ground pretty damn quick and covered himself up like the way I used to when Daddy got mad at me.

There was one time, not long before his death, I caught him looking in the mirror wearing Mom's dress and heels. He was blowing himself kisses and stuff and he saw me and he got real mad. He wiped the lipstick off his face and threw off the high heels and started taking off the dress as he chased me through the hallways.

"Don't you dare tell your mom, you little shit!" he would say. I could smell the liquor on him when he yelled. I ran through the house, trying to figure out why I'd ever tell anybody. I didn't care what he was up to. He liked floral prints and hurting his feet for some unobtainable standard of beauty; why would I lose sleep over it?

"Don't tell your mom, you hear me!? I'll kill you! I'll kill my goddamn self!"

Ain't ever thought about it in a long time, though. Hard to think about when you're trying to escape a secret government facility.

I couldn't hit somebody cowering like that, anyways.

"You were just doing your job," I said and turned around for the weirdo in the top hat. I'm going to call him Gold Tooth because his teeth were all capped in gold as I mentioned earlier.

"Where is the dummy hiding?" I called out because I wanted him to know exactly what I thought of him; he was a dumb ass who used big words to hide the fact that he was full of goddamn shit just like every damn therapist I've ever been to. Take a drug for that, take a drug for this, you're depressed, you're delusional, your dad was an asshole, what's your relationship like with your mother, why are all the women in your life throwing you out? Put a sock in it, nerds. I know who I am and I know who I'll always be. I ain't always been him but then one fateful night I got shot in the face over a goddamn pickled egg and I lived to rename myself Bangface. I'm Bangface, dammit, and no amount of CIA glory hole experiment is going to change that.

"Don't be so sure," the intercom voice returned. "Tee-hee."

"Why say tee-hee? Why not just giggle? And how can you hear my thoughts?"

"We can hear your thoughts for precisely the same reason you can sense the subtle changes in our universe. We shot you, motherfucker."

That was pretty unprofessional even by American government standards. Totally unnecessary. Maybe that's why the Russians hate us so much. We go around calling people motherfuckers.

"You're telling me there was some kind of plan this whole time? One of your stooges came into a bar and got into a fight over the last pickled egg with me?"

"That's how it played out in one universe, yes. Did it play out in this one? You're a Sense Being but you can only sense what you've already known. Your past is constantly changing and now we know where we can mold you into the perfect test subject."

I didn't understand any of this shit and I suspect none of you do, either. That's bureaucracy for you folks. Red tape, Sense Beings, committees… the list goes on. I've had enough of it, though. I sensed a whimpering coming from under the dick examining table they put me on. It was Gold Tooth, trying one of my tricks by pissing himself.

"I don't slip and slide so easy, amigo," I said right before I lost my footing on the tile floor he pissed on. It was perfect timing for such arrogance. That's what the universe does, though. You think you know something and all the sudden the menu changes the next time you're at the drive thru. Tacos at Burger King? There ain't a universe that that makes sense in. I'm sorry, folks, I'd had just about enough of all this hocus pocus.

My tailbone hurt pretty bad and I could feel the pain reverberating through my whole body. Gold Tooth still was shivering underneath the table.

"I have a secret," he said. "I'm a test subject, too."

I had to kick him in the nose just once because I did slip in his pee and you gotta let folks know that you don't put up with that.

"What do you mean by that?"

"I mean, they told me that if I didn't help them find other Sense Beings they were going to throw me in the looney bin and ruin my credit. One thing is enough but both? Man, they can get real ugly here at the CIA. I told them I'd do whatever they wanted."

"So you sit around looking at pee holes in wieners all day?"

"They are a thorough bunch, these goons."

I don't know why I believed him but I did. He looked familiar aside from all the gold teeth. I couldn't put my finger on it.

"You look familiar," he said interrupting my own epiphany. "I feel like I might have shot someone who looked a lot like you, except his face wasn't as fucked up as yours was."

"You motherfucker," I said and grabbed him by the nose and threw him up at the ceiling. I could hear his back break in a couple different places before he fell back to the floor and flattened out.

But then I sensed pink smoke flowing from underneath the door into the operating room and all of the sudden, the menu changed if you know what I mean. All of the sudden, Gold Tooth didn't look familiar and, in this universe at least, I may have done some permanent damage to an innocent man.

Fuck, y'all. My head hurts.

EIGHTEEN

There was lights flashing all red and lots of beeping noises. A voice on the intercom kept saying, "All units on alert! All units on alert! This is not a drill!"

But most of the unit in my room was on the floor, knocked out and probably dying. Sleeping on the job. That's government bureaucracy for you. They'll raise your taxes to take more naps. That's not how it works in the private world at all, folks. I've been on both sides. Now that I own my own business I work much harder for way less but I at least get the dignity to look down on the pecker pushers in the CIA. I bet mailmen work real hard, though.

Gold Tooth was on the floor passed out like he had just turned 21; in a puddle of his own piss and vomit. I took off his lab coat and buttoned it top to bottom. I didn't expect too much from the government workers in here to notice that I wasn't wearing shoes. I'd be able to slip by, no problemo. The door was unlocked. Amateurs.

I opened it and peeked down the hall that stretched both ways. When I was a kid, Daddy always said, "Right is right," but I heard from somebody recently say, "Left is law." That's the problem with our geographically contextual directions folks. My right is your left so either one of us could be wrong according to these phrases. People should learn cardinal directions. I hear there are these tribes out in the middle of nowhere that don't have any words for right or left. Instead, like pigeons – fucking birds, folks! – they have compass directions hardwired into their brains. They don't say, "Turn left when you see the slobbering dog atop Crazy Bill's knee." They say, "A slobbering dog will be on Crazy Bill's knee to the north about five clicks. From there, head east for five clicks."

I don't really know, though. I was born in America, dammit. An inch is an inch and a left hand turn could be in any damn compass direction. And that's the way I like and that's the way it should be because everything different is weird and vaguely communistic. We all know that the Reds were up to no good. I can't even root for a team as all American as the Boston Red Sox. I can't vote Republican because they're the red states. I was taught real good but these days I can't even tell if the Communists are still around or if they're not. China's so scary because they're so good at the game we set up for them.

"Where the Hell do you think you're going?"

It was Vince.

"You know, Vincent, my friend, it's a funny thing. When you came into my office, I felt bad for you. I've been cheated on and abused and plenty of women have left me for better made silicon dildos. It hurts when a bathroom stall has more gravitas than a human being. I felt for you, I really did. I'd been in your shoes. But now I can see why your lover left you. You're a cold man who, honestly, is far less desirable than a dirty trucker's toilet stall. Less desirable than a crude, serrated, hole in the bathroom stall at that! Just standing here talking to you makes me want to fuck the nearest toilet."

I got up real close to him and put my mouth real close to his nose because I could taste how bad my breath stank and I wanted him to be as uncomfortable as possible.

"You know where the Hell I think I'm going, dummy? I'm going to get my woman back and then I'm going to save this country from itself all by my damn self because Daddy always said, 'Ain't nothing needs fixin' until it's broken,' and God dammit, it's broken."

Vince cowered away from me. He pulled out some Tic Tacs.

"Toc Tuck?" he asked me as he opened the case.

"Jesus diddlin' Christ. You're really fucking shit up with these glory holes, bucko!"

I gave him a good punch to the mouth and he fell, spilling all of his Toc Tucks.

"You bastard," he yelled. "That was my last pack of banarange flavor!"

Folks, this whole damn world was getting topsy turvy and I could feel my stomach get pretty strong emotions. I wanted to throw up is what I'm trying to say. I kicked him the face. It was barefoot so don't worry too much about how mean it is to kick someone in the face. Probably just broke his nose.

"Give me your pants."

"What?" He looked up at me with his nose about two inches further to the left than it used to be. I could practically see the birds flying in circles above his head.

I didn't bother asking again. You don't take a man's pants when he's seeing stars. They did it to me but two wrongs don't make a right, folks. You just remember that. This, from now on, was a freeballing sneaking mission.

"You don't understand..." Vince said as he choked

on his own consciousness. "We need you…"

Nobody ever told me they needed me before. I gotta admit, folks, this struck me in the kind of way that made me want to break down and cry.

"We need more Sense Beings to document the subtle changes in our universe so we can change them all back once our technology is perfected. We need as many Sense Beings as possible." Then he passed out.

I filed that away and put it in my mental back pocket. I still had a woman to see and my John Dangler needed the support of pants or boxers or tighty whiteys or, hell, a sock. I'm no exhibitionist, ladies and gentlemen. Y'all just go on doing what makes you happy but I was getting tired of flopping around.

And I needed a Topo Chico.

NINETEEN

Some folks think Texas is nothing but cowboys shooting rabbits and eating cactus in the heat. Nothing but sand and wind and oil refineries. Humidity and hostility. Sometimes it gets cold, folks. Today was one of those days. I was sneaking around the CIA parking lot, jumping behind cars and holding my pecker and acorns in my hands. People must've thought I was crazy but if only they'd give me a chance to explain, they'd know I ain't.

But they never gave me a chance.

"Excuse me, miss? I need a ride downtown, real quick, my lady is expecting me and the government took all my clothes and this fucking lab coat is chafing my nipples like I just ran a marathon."

She slapped me and locked her door. I don't blame her. I never picked up a just-about-nude fella. Never saw one asking for a ride but wouldn't if I did.

"Hey, cowboy!" I waved at some teenager pointing his cellphone at me and giggling. "Let me use your phone, I gotta call my lady and, boy, you know how they get when you don't call them." I made the crazy fingers at my head and crossed my eyes and stuck out my tongue. "They get cuckoo."

The kid kept giggling.

"You're gonna go viral, bro," he said.

I've been tested, amigos. I've been tested after every sexual encounter with a strange woman. I've been tested after I shook some questionable hands, too. I wasn't viral and I sure as hell ain't going to go viral now. I had already banked it in my mind that I was going to get tested after my Enola Gay rubbed the fabrics of this lab coat a little too intimately.

It's all about responsibility. That's something that's lost today. Daddy always said to own up to your mistakes and make sure you don't make them too often. I knew a guy with gonorrhea before and he was telling me he was sneezing out of his dickhole. It sounded none too pleasant. I'm not about that noise, folks. I sneeze out of my nose, I spit out of my mouth, and I piss out of my slugger. That's how God intended and that's how I intend to honor Him.

I ain't too religious, though. Some folks go crazy for that stuff. You have to wonder if man was made in God's image, then God must be a wiener like the rest of us.

Anyway, I charged the kid with the phone and grabbed it out of his hand.

"Yo, man, you're gonna have to pay for that."

"I don't have to pay for anything. This is America. I need something so I'm going to take it. Ever hear of an hombre by the name of George W. Bush?"

"That guy was a fascist."

"To you, squirt. You were nothing but a tingle in your pappy's scrotum when he was first elected. You're lucky you didn't get flushed down the shitter during one of your dad's late night shit n' strokes."

"What's your fucking deal, man?"

"My deal is I have to see my lady before she turns into a man or a dog or a fast food joint. The fabric of our universe is in flux right now, not that you'd ever understand it."

The little shit was filming me. I should have known but I don't know these things. I come from a simpler time of beepers and AOL Instant Messenger. Back in the good old days when the internet came on CDs with a set amount of free hours. The wild west days, folks, when websites had really long names and mouse tails. Those were the days. I can't imagine having a phone stuck in my palm all day long. We sat at a computer to jerk off to the only porn site we knew of; Playboy.com. And when we heard the footsteps of my folks coming back home from fighting in the park, we'd take the power cord between our toes and pop it out of socket.

We went through a lot of computers.

"I just need to dial my old lady, kid."

"Sure, man, whatever."

I dialed 4-1-1 because, though I proclaim the virtues of being a luddite, I don't have to remember numbers thanks to American progress.

"Operator here, who are you calling?"

"I need my old lady!"

"Sir, I need a name."

"Fucking shit, I have to go. No wonder your industry is doomed." I threw the little shit's phone on the ground and started running in the direction I thought I should be going. I wasn't sure but I figured once I got out onto a main street, I'd find my way. They used to call me the homing device back on the force. I could find my way out of anything. Couldn't find my way out of a bullet's path, though.

"You fucker! You broke my fucking phone! My mom's going to kill me!"

I heard the little shit screaming but it was go time,

folks. It'd been awhile since I'd seen my lady and if the universe was shifting so much she might've forgotten she hated me. Nothing in the world worse than having your woman hate you. She goes and dials her sisters long distance and cries into the phone for hours while the soup gets cold. Just like mom used to do. She stopped talking after pa did what he did. In her dress and high heels, nonetheless. Must've been tough. I like my soup cold, though.

TWENTY

She opened the door and stared at me almost like I was invisible to her. She didn't say anything. She just moved to the side as if to say, "Okay, come in." Except she didn't say anything besides a sigh.

The TV was on. It was on some ladies' show where they discuss the latest celebrity zit and what the President ate for the cameras that one day. It was too loud.

"Can you turn it down?" I said. "I've had a long day."

She didn't say a word. She got up and turned the TV off. Then she plopped back down onto the couch and stared into but right past my face.

"You know," I said. "It's been quite a while."

"Shut up," she said.

I can smell a pregnant lady just two weeks after she's blasted. They smell rubbery and salty and my old lady smelled real rubbery. But you can tell a pregnant lady mostly by the way she treats the man who popped one in her shithouse. Real mean and impatient-like… and my lady was being real mean.

"I'm pregnant," she said.

"I knew it! I could smell it on you as soon as you opened the door. It was like a wall of burnt rubber hit me right in the nostrils as soon as I saw you. All pregnant ladies smell like that. You can't always trust your eyes. You gained a lot of weight since the last time I stuck the baster in the turkey. How long has it been?"

"You're not the father."

She was being real mean, now. So mean she went around claiming I wasn't the daddy. Come on, folks. I knew her and she was a good Christian girl. Never fucked more than her own fingers before she met me. Now she's claiming I ain't the pops? Come on.

"You ain't been home in two fucking years, you idiot."

"You ever hear of a guy named Jesus?"

"Get out."

"Well, who's the daddy then?"

"Jerry."

"Big Man Japan?"

Big Man Japan. The backstabbing Oriental. I know you're not supposed to say that anymore but I was mad and I didn't mean anything by it. I can't call him a Chinaman because he's Japanese and if you know anything about the Chinese and the Japanese, it's that they really hate each other.

"Big Man Japan?" she asked.

"You probably didn't know this, sweetcheeks, but we used to call him Big Man Japan because he went to Japan and because he's a half-breed and all he towered over everyone there. You should get to know your sexual partners a little better before you run off starting families."

I shook my fucking head because it couldn't take much more news from whatever universe I was living in now. She knew Jerry was called Big Man Japan. I coined the damn term and I talked about it every night before we went to bed just so she knew that I was capable of being clever just like all the other guys she giggled with at work.

You can't give anyone your heart, folks. You get kicked out and blamed for not coming home after two years.

"Well, you kicked me out!" I said as if my argument in my head was with her.

"You were drinking so much you were fucking bottles of Jack Daniels, Rogeli-"

"I don't go by that name anymore, you know that. I'm a junior to no man. Not even my daddy. The pussy hung himself because he liked wearing lady clothes. I get it, I get it. It was a different time back then but just imagine if he'd've stuck around? Guess he wouldn't be a granddad, though. He'd be drinking with me and eating pickled eggs at the bar while we talked about Big Man Japan and the Kid That Should Have Been Mine."

"You should go."

She tried to put her arm around my shoulder but I brushed it away.

"Yeah, lady, I know. Tell Big Man Japan I say hello and congratulations and you can go fuck yourself, missus."

TWENTY ONE

I ain't ever been much closer to relapsing back into the bottle than I was right after that. I was still wearing the lab coat, freeballing, and it was cold. Whiskey always warmed my bones.

There was a hole in the wall Mexican food joint just down the street that used to be my old pissing hole. With any luck, it'd still be a Mexican food joint and not some Italian kind of place.

There wasn't much left to do, anyways. What else could I change about the government fucking the world up with some pie in the sky thinking about a high speed traveling machine? If they wanted to build it or bomb it, they would. We don't have the draft anymore so Americans don't feel connected to whatever pooch their government is screwing. Daddy always said ending the draft was the worst decision Congress ever made. He was in Vietnam, too. He knew what he was talking about. He was a Nixon man. Nixon gets a bad rap but your opinions on Nixon are already hardened and I figure it's best not to try to change an ass's mind, anyhow.

When I got in, not one person said a word about my getup. They recognized me.

"Bangface! Come in! Come in!"

"You're still Marta, no?"

"Of course, you idiot."

"I'll have some chips and salsa and…" I stared at their healthy selection of Topo Chico and Budweiser and whiskey. "Get me a shot of whiskey, a Topo Chico, and a whole fucking six pack of Budweiser."

They don't call it the King of Beers for nothing, amigo. You can drink a whole six pack and not feel drunk until you have to stand up to go and then you gotta sit back down because you're in no position to walk. It happens, folks. Used to happen to me all the damn time. Sometimes I wouldn't sit back down and I'd go home and fuck a bottle of Jack. Those were the bad nights.

"Bangface, you can't do that anymore. You told me never to let you order alcohol again and then you never came back."

I lifted my face off the table and said, "Well, baby, I'm back."

"I don't like you like this."

"What's it to you, anyways? Treat me like any other customer."

"TABC law states I can serve two drinks maximum to any one individual at a time. While I'd be happy to give you a whole six pack in my home, I can only grab you a shot and one Bud."

"Make it a tall boy, then."

The chips and salsa came first. They always come first. They want to pucker your lips up and dry out your mouth so bad that you can't help but take a gander at their margarita menu. I knew what I wanted, though.

As I munched on their homemade tortilla chips (huge difference, you'll never go back to Tostitos after this place), a man in a dark trench coat, sunglasses, and a fedora came in. Marta looked like she recognized him. He looked like a goon and I was in no mood for goons. I'd'd've had a goddamned 'nuff of them. I lowered my eyes and stared at my salsa long enough to the point I had to piss.

I got up and went to the toilet. First stall. A glory hole. A nice one, too. It was gold plated and it had a serial number on it. I stuck my finger through it and, sure enough, it poked some goon in the eye on the other side. A goon in a cubicle, staring at a computer.

"Ow! My fucking eye!" he said.

"Try getting shot in the face, Chicken Breath!"

I hawked a loogie at him through the glory hole with my lips getting uncomfortably close to it. I'd schedule a test as soon as this shenanigans was done.

"What the fuck was that for?"

I didn't pay him any attention. I stepped out of the bathroom renewed.

"Marta, get me a Topo Chico right now and explain what the hell a glory hole is doing in your pisser!"

The man in black was staring at me.

"That's him," he said.

"They paid me a lot of money to be a transport site, Bangface!"

"Shut up," the man in black said.

"Don't you talk to her that way. You're in her house, poncho!"

The man took off his hat and took off his shades and his trench coat. He was wearing a Hawaiian shirt.

"You're all in it together, ain't you? You and Vince! This was all some complicated trap for me to eat the cheese in, wasn't it?"

"You're coming with me, Bangface."

"Marta, take no more of their money. Soon your store will be a Starbucks below a condo and you'll never remember what it was."

Marta looked at me cross eyed like I was stupid. I was getting real tired of that look.

"Come with me, Bangface," the man said.

"I'll go, I'll go," I said. I put my hands in the air like I was surrendering but a fake surrender is the best way to get a quick kick to the nutsack. I read it in the Art of War. That Chinaman was pretty damn smart when it came to winning wars, large and small. If your enemy is irritable, irritate him. Ain't nothing more irritating than clutching your nutsack as it turns into a pussy.

He fell to the floor in pain but three more black coated men came in and carried me right back into the pisser. They took off my pants and stuck my sticker into the hole. I disappeared into a cloud of pink smoke with my dick out standing right in front of the guy I spit at in his government cubicle.

"Nice mug." I pointed to his 'I Hate Mondays' mug. "What day is it?"

"Mo-"

I kicked him the face. "Shut up. I know what day it is."

TWENTY TWO

When the guy was done cleaning the blood off of his nose and popping it back into place he pointed to his computer.

"Take a look at this. You want to know the answer to your grand mystery, don't you? You want to know who shot you in the face, don't you?"

He floored me with that. Of course I did. I've been wondering that for damn near a decade.

"Because you've been able to point out so many inconsistencies for us, Vince decided it was time to show you."

He clicked around on some files and a video started playing. It was real blurry and pink.

"We are now able to backtrack in time and record moments to preserve history so that we can get the past back to what it was."

"I don't understand a damn thing you said."

"Anyways." His nose started bleeding again. He

clicked play.

It was me, outside the bar, screaming in the fetal position on the sidewalk.

"I don't remember that. I don't cry much."

There was silence in the room.

"Well, I don't."

There I was, though, screaming like a baby just born and pulling out my own gun and pointing it at my own face.

"Turn it off," I said. "There's no way to be sure that's real."

"You're a Sense Being. You'd know if it was fake."

Truth is, folks, I didn't know anything. Once I pointed my gun, I always hit my mark.

"If that was real, I'd be dead as a dingleberry right now."

"Are you willing to work with us? We can change the past permanently for you." It was Vince. He put his hand on my shoulder.

It didn't matter who shot me in the face be it me or Gold Tooth or anyone else. The past was always changing depending on how you looked at it.

"Hell, no I ain't working with the feds."

I could feel the cold steel of handcuffs clasping around my wrists and then the click.

"You're working with us whether you want to or not. You can't stand in the way of progress."

Sure, I could. I could piss and shit all over this office if I wanted and I could gum up the works by talking and talking and talking. But it was no damn use.

TWENTY THREE

Surely, you didn't think it was over. I ate the gruel they served me for a few weeks and worked my eyeballs all over the videos they showed me every time a fed stuck his pecker in a peeper. I noted the differences.

Daddy always said take your work seriously and do it the best you could because there was always someone else in line with a boner for your job. And this is America, you'll get replaced for some foggy eyed college graduate for half the pay.

Half of zero still is nothing, though folks.

We were huddled around a steel table, me and the other Sense Beings one day when the foreman came in and asked to take our orders from MacDonald's.

"I'll have a chocolate shake, some French fries, and a Big Mac," I said. "And, fuck it, let's get some

McNuggets, too."

The foreman looked at me like I was stupid. Like I said, I was getting real tired of that look.

"Repeat your order, retard," he told me.

I don't take too kindly to people using slurs like that, especially when they're throwing them at me.

"Jimbo," I said, "why don't you grab yourself a pen and write this down." I started to speak real slow-like just so the bozo would get it right. "I want a chocolate shake, French fries, a Big Mac, and some chicken McNuggets."

"Where do you think you're ordering from?"

"I'm ordering from goddamned McDonald's and I'm a Sense Being so I know what's what, dummy."

"It's MacDonald's."

Shit needed fixing, folks. For all the hard labor they forced me to do spotting differences and all that, something as simple as McDonald's name not being changed was a goddamned travesty. I bet you Andrew Jackson ain't even on the twenty in this stupid, good for nothing universe.

"It ain't MacDonald's, it never was, and if I have anything to do with it, it never will be!"

I flipped the steel table over and hit Gold Tooth right in the head. His face split open right down the middle and he was spouting blood all over the place. All the other Sense Beings stood up and put their backs against the wall.

"I said I was going to find the man who shot me in the face and kill him," I said. "I said I was going to make him pay but now I find out, thanks to the federal government, that I may have shot my own damn face off. Well, I'm going to die trying to make things right, dammit."

If something's wrong, you fix it. Daddy said that, too.

The other Sense Beings were cowering in the corner like a bunch of Democrats in the face of danger. I lunged for the foreman, grabbed his hair, and started banging his head against the floor. If I had an ounce of piss in me, I'd piss all over the place, too, because that seems to do wonders around this place.

It was easy to get out of the room. It was right around clocking out time for all the contract workers here and, if you know anything about government workers, they don't lift a finger on the clock... why would they lift a finger off?

"Good night, Miranda," I said to one of the secretaries who was on her way out.

"Good night," she said, not even looking up from her phone to see who greeted her. I told you; government goons. But it ain't just government goons, it's the whole damn world. Everywhere you go folks got their noses to their phones going cross eyed trying to figure out who still likes them. I used to try to figure that out, too. Used to drive me crazy. But it ain't conducive to production and everyone knows that Americans work harder than the whole world ten times over. Leave paternity leave to the French. My old lady's pregnant and I'm here working overtime trying to figure out whether or not a street is named Parker or Porker.

There was a million which ways I could go. There was the lady in the muumuu. There was the sleaze ball lawyer office neighbor. There was my cat, Mariposa, who – come to think of it- probably needed to be fed. There was the numbers station to listen to. There was Big Man Japan.

I don't make plans. I make connections. And none of this made any kind of goddamned sense. I just had to get to Vince.

Lucky for me, all this thinking about what to do next slammed me right into Vince's chest.

"Where do you think you're going?"

"I can't take it anymore. The McDonald's thing is killing me. I place an order and nothing I order is on the damn menu. It goes deeper than just Mc becoming Mac, doc!"

"Keep working. We'll fix it all."

I'd been working my ass off and there wasn't a damn sign of change anywhere. I was the teenager cleaning toilets again.

"I quit."

"You can't quit. You're an agent of the federal government."

"You take that back, bucko. You take that back. I don't work for the government."

"Yes, you do." Vince pulled out a badge with my picture on it. Sure enough, it had my given name and it said "Federal Employee" right under it.

"I don't go by that name."

"Then you should have had it legally changed."

All of this bureaucracy, all of this red tape, all of this nonsense. A man should be able to go by whatever he wants to go by. A man should be whatever he wants to be. A man shouldn't have to be a federal employee.

I didn't even think it, folks, I swear. It just happened. I did my patented bicycle kick compliments of Villareal taekwondo. My foot connected to his chin and I heard a crack. He fell to the floor, unconscious. He wasn't dead. I checked his pulse just to make sure. I don't go around killing people. I go around getting answers and when there ain't answers, I go around nearly killing people.

There weren't no other employees around so I dragged Vince into the nearest supply closet and locked the door. I walked out. Free as ice.

TWENTY
FOUR

I looked like an escaped prisoner wearing a white jumpsuit but I had a mission. There was a MacDonald's not too far away from here. I walked. And as I walked I was screaming.

"Y'all know just what the fuck is going on here? Your government is testing a high speed transport system that changes little details about the universe every damn time it's used. You see a glory hole? Patch it up! Don't stick your slugger in it!"

It was good advice regardless of the current conspiratorial circumstances. Why'd anyone stick their intimates into a hole cut out from particle board is beyond me but I personally can't get aroused so close to a pooper or a pisser. I've caught some folks in the heat of passion steaming up public restrooms but they were always wrapped around each other not one getting their knees all dirty and banging their head against a stall while the other stands up, pants 'round his ankles, moaning never seeing who's on the other side. It just doesn't make any sense to me but this is the United States and you can do whatever the hell you want so long as you ain't caught.

"MacDonald's is a lie!" I yelled as I walked up to MacDonald's. "It's McDonald's! And I don't know what they serve here but if it ain't Big Macs and McNuggets, it ain't McDonald's folks!"

"Son, close your eyes. Some people are just less fortunate than we are," some dad said to his kid.

"You're damn right some are less fortunate. I was forced to watch hours and hours of video trying to spot small changes in the structure of our damn universe while you were slurping on a McFlurry or whatever the hell they call it here."

"I'm going to call the cops."

"Go for it. Call the cops! I don't care! At least in prison I'll be treated like a damn person!"

It was probably also my best bet. I was on the force once, remember? Every time there was a jurisdictional disagreement between the locals and the feds, the feds would puff up their chests and stop talking to us.

There was a puff of pink smoke around the roof of the MacDonald's.

"Look at that, you Neanderthal! You see that pink smoke? That means some pervert used a glory hole and something about the universe has changed. Maybe your taint ain't hairy anymore. Maybe your son is a daughter now. Maybe your wife doesn't love you, your daddy committed suicide, and you just found out you shot your own damn face off!"

The kid started crying. Kids these days. I tell you what. I've taken physical abuse and verbal abuse and I can tell you which I prefer and it definitely ain't the kind that leaves bruises and broken legs and the kind that makes your mom hide underneath the kitchen table and your brother run away for three days staying at some church while daddy cooled off. I could take verbal abuse. That ain't shit.

There were sirens, of course. Somebody else called the cops. I'd probably call the cops on me, too.

"You're coming with us."

They handcuffed me. They kicked me. They spit on me. The kids did. But as they lowered my head to get into the back of the car, I took one look at that fast food restaurant.

By God, it said McDonald's.

ABOUT THE AUTHOR

Andrew Hilbert lives and works in Austin, TX. He is the author of *Death Thing*, published by Double Life Press, *Cat Food*, and *Toilet Stories From Outer Space*, published by Weekly Weird Monthly. You can keep up with all he's doing at http://www.hilbertheckler.com or by following him on Facebook, or Twitter/Instagram at @AHILBERT3000.